THE DAY SONNY DIED

THE DAY SONNY DIED

M. Simone Boyd

and

Onnie I. Kirk, Jr.

eGenCo

Generation Culture Transformation
Specializing in publishing for generation culture change

eGenCo

eGenCo
824 Tallow Hill Road
Chambersburg, PA 17202, USA
Phone: 717-461-3436
Email: info@egen.co
Website: www.egen.co

facebook.com/egenbooks

youtube.com/egenpub

egen.co/blog

pinterest.com/eGenDMP

twitter.com/eGenDMP

instagram.com/egenco_dmp

Publisher's Cataloging-in-Publication Data
Boyd, M. Simone and Onnie I. Kirk, Jr.
The Day Sonny Died.; by M. Simone Boyd and Onnie I.
Kirk, Jr. Rebekah Helman, editor.
194 pages cm.
ISBN: 978-1-68019-828-7 paperback
        978-1-68019-829-4 ebook
        978-1-68019-830-0 ebook
1. Murder. 2. Family generational curse. 3. Religion.
I. Title
2016952580

For you, My Darling...

Pure religion and undefiled before God and the Father is this,
to visit the fatherless and widows in their affliction,
and to keep himself unspotted from the world.

James 1:27

TABLE OF CONTENTS

CHAPTER ONE

There was still blood on Sonny's shoes when the detective came to interview him. Constance could barely keep him on her lap, much less change his soiled clothes. Even the creak of her rocking chair on the hardwood floor could not be heard above his constant screaming— "Da-da! Da-da!" His nose was running, and his arms were flailing.

Constance tried with all her might to contain his three-year-old body, but Sonny was shrieking and kicking as if he'd been set on fire. Pointing. Clawing. Anything he could do to get out of his grandmother's lap and back onto the street with his dad.

Victor Junior's body lay outside on the sidewalk covered by a police tarpaulin. But despite the feeling of death that hung in the air, Constance kept calm. Courtesy of all those days of enduring Victor Senior, she was accustomed to pushing down her emotions and maintaining resolve during chaos.

Even so, a solitary tear had managed to escape from her eye, one that Constance wiped with the corner of her floral apron. *Well,* she thought, *at least I won't have to worry about Victor Junior anymore.* Her worst fear of what could happen to her one and only son had come and gone.

She'd been in the kitchen baking an apple pie when three loud cracks had split the neighborhood's Saturday morning chatter. Gun shots. They were closer this time, and something had clicked in her heart when she heard the sounds.

Constance remembered stepping out onto the sidewalk, and from that moment, everything seemed to move in slow motion. The screams, the neighbors running, and three-year-old Sonny standing there beside his brand-new bike, next to his dad lying lifeless on the pavement.

A neighbor then placed Sonny in Constance's arms, and a detective came into her living room with his dirty boots, sat on her Victorian settee, and proceeded to ask a litany of routine questions. But Constance couldn't remember a word she'd said to him.

"Sonny...Sonny! Sit still." Constance held Sonny's face with both hands and stared into his eyes. "Listen to me...*listen*. He is *not* coming back." She said flatly.

Sonny's screams quieted to a whimper as he gasped for air and tried to free his head from his grandmother's grip. But Constance forced his head on her shoulder and began to hum "Blessed Assurance" over the sound of his sobs.

She retraced the last few years in her memory, and for a few moments, she relived the day that changed everything. From then on, it had been a slow march to this end, and now Victor Junior had joined the rest of the Jackson men in the afterlife.

* * *

Three and a half years earlier, Rachel Marie Andrews sat crossed-legged on the floor of the mint green bathroom next to the pastor's study and wiped away the tears mixed with mascara running down her face. She gripped the handful of pills and reassured herself that this would get her parents' attention—this time.

She always felt forced to compete for her parents' time. Just last week, when she'd asked her mother for ten dollars to pay for school pictures, her mother hadn't even looked up from her Sunday school lesson. "Get it out of my purse," she instructed absentmindedly. Rachel couldn't even remember the last time her mother had made dinner for her. She was always too busy or too tired from dealing with church business.

Rachel thought about what her dad would say when he found his sweet baby girl slightly blue and lifeless. He would be devastated—and that's what he deserved. But he would think about the good times too. A gentle smile spread across Rachel's lips as she remembered her second-grade dance recital.

She'd been selected for a solo and practiced until she drove her parents crazy. But during the recital, she froze, and the dance routine she knew backwards and forwards was erased from her memory. Rachel stood there like an ice queen in her leotard and black, patent-leather tap shoes, then bit her lip and tried to choke back the tears.

Before one tear could fall though, her dad had jumped up onto the stage and filled in the parts she'd missed. The step, cross, kick-jazz-hands, cross, and kick were executed, and then her father spun around and offered his hand. They finished the entire routine like that's the way they had always planned it.

The crowd of parents and grandparents leapt to their feet and clapped as if it was her Broadway debut. Her dad looked at her and smiled. In his fatherly way, he had picked Rachel up and saved her dance solo.

"But he won't be here to pick me up this time," Rachel whispered as she let out a sigh and thought about the positive pregnancy test she'd taken at school. As she used her free hand to grab the bathroom sink and pull herself up from the floor, she leaned over to get a better look in the mirror and decided that her lipstick needed to be freshened. She wanted to look pretty when her parents found her.

Rachel fumbled through her makeup bag and fished out her princess-pink lipstick. She thought about all the sermons her dad had preached on forgiveness and love but was sure that none of that would apply when he found out that his sixteen-year-old daughter was pregnant. No, she couldn't face him. He would explode. So, she would finish everything here...in her own way.

Don't do this, she heard.

Rachel straightened her dress and took a deep breath. She counted the pills in her hand, then wiped her mouth before she angled her head to get one last swig from the bathroom faucet. But just as she started to lean down, she stopped to take another look in the mirror.

There draped around her neck, she noticed the butterfly necklace that Victor Junior had given her as a sixteenth birthday present. She gripped it between her fingers and brought it up to her lips. Maybe she should talk to Victor Junior. He would know what to do.

* * *

The shrill of Coach Grime's whistle signaled the end of another Wednesday basketball practice. Sweaty teenage bodies took in a collective inhale and tried to catch up with their breath.

"Bring it in, guys—that's it for today." Coach Grimes positioned his clipboard on his waist, noticeably fuming while the team gathered around at a snail's pace.

"Most of y'all weren't even here today," he let his glare rest on Victor Junior, the team captain. "So you're going to make up for it tomorrow. Practice before and after school."

The team groaned, and someone elbowed Victor Junior in the ribs.

"Let's go. Lions on three," Coach Grimes directed.

"One-two-three—Lions," the team responded without enthusiasm.

Drained, the circle broke up and the boys headed toward the locker room. But Victor Junior hung back and fell into step with Coach Grimes.

"Coach, can I talk to you for a minute?"

"Yeah...what is it?" Coach Grimes paused for a second to look at him and took off his cap to scratch his head. He'd invested so much time in this boy, but it was clear that Victor Junior was just going through the motions. He'd missed four free-throws in warm-ups alone and had barely kept up with the other guys during practice.

"Kind-a personal. Could I come to your office?"

Coach Grimes inhaled, nodded, and pulled out his office keys. *Well, at least the boy recognized his game was off today.*

Victor Junior followed the older man to his office and waited while he jangled his ring of keys to get the office door open. *Why does Coach lock that door anyway* wondered Victor, *when there ain't nothing in that office but uniforms and practice equipment?*

Coach Grimes swung the door open and nodded for Victor Junior to go on in and have a seat. Victor Junior watched Coach as he moved the folders piled up on his desk and said a silent prayer that Rachel could come to Chapel Hill with him. Maybe they could even get married and move into an apartment on campus.

Coach Grimes finished rearranging the papers on his desk, interlaced his fingers and leaned toward him. "Well?"

Victor Junior cleared his throat, looked down at the practice jersey he was wearing, and pulled it away from his chest. "Rachel's pregnant, and I need to figure things out."

Coach Grimes let out a slow sigh and rubbed his temples. Victor Junior sat in the silence and waited.

"Have you told Constance?" He looked down at his desk.

"Nah, not yet."

"This will kill her."

"I know," Victor Junior scratched his forearm and tried to force his mother's face from his mind.

"How could you do this, Vic? How could you be so stupid? You were ten months away from putting on whatever jersey you wanted. God, I just..."

"Me and Rach could get married? You know...and maybe...get an apartment on campus? I could still play."

"No. It doesn't work like that."

"What d'ya mean?"

"It doesn't work like that. Just because you are a good ball player doesn't guarantee you a spot on a team. The margin for error is so slim, Victor Junior. You know that. We've talked about this a thousand..."

"...times. I know, Coach. *I know*. There's a lot of good ball players. You have to be the total package—ball, brains, and a clean record."

"Well, why didn't you listen?" Coach Grimes slammed his fist on the desk. "You were this close. This close," he held his fingers up in the air for emphasis. "No team is going to touch a married freshman with his underaged wife. Imagine the headlines. Too much of a distraction. Basketball at that level is a business, and that's what you'd be—nothing but a liability."

He'd spent years on trying to get this boy out of that house with his dad and on his way to a good college and to another coach who would look out for him. Coach Grimes had even taken him to summer basketball camps on his own dime. Made phone calls and written letters just so he'd have the right team at the right time when Victor Junior was ready to make a commitment.

5

But ten months away from suiting up for a D-I, Victor Junior was throwing it all away. He tapped his knuckles on the desk and looked the young man squarely in the eyes.

"So…now that basketball is off the table, what are you going to do?"

Victor Junior sat under Coach Grimes glare for a second and then looked off.

"I dunno," he shrugged.

"The first thing you need to do is tell your mother. Do her parents know?"

"Nah, not yet."

Pastor Andrews is really gonna hit the roof, thought Coach. *But Constance. Constance. She's worked so hard to keep her family together. To get her boy to this point. This is gonna kill her.*

"Let me go with you to tell your mother."

"No, I want to handle it myself," Victor Junior moved to the edge of his chair and looked up.

"Coach, I'm sorry. You wanted this as much as I did. And I let you down too."

Coach Grimes tried to still the feelings pushing up through his chest, but they were already on the move. "Let's just make the best of this season," his voice cracked as he got up from his desk, and moved around to pat Victor Junior on the shoulder.

The pat collapsed into a hug.

"Don't let this one mistake define you, son. You still got a lot of choices and a lot of life ahead of you, okay?"

CHAPTER TWO

C onstance Elizabeth Jackson noticed the fingerprints on the sliding glass doors at the entrance of Kroger. No matter what time of day she came to the store, the fingerprints were always present and accounted for, which made her wonder about the cleanliness of the store's food management practices.

But this was the only grocery store within a five-mile radius of their home that Victor let her go to alone. In recent years, he'd become more and more paranoid that she'd up and leave. It'd been almost 25 years since they'd married, but he was still convinced she might take off at any moment.

He should have remembered, though, that Constance would have never let her son grow up without his father. Besides, she'd made a vow before God...'til death. She'd thought once or twice about helping to speed up the process, but Victor Junior needed his father—regardless of her husband's shortcomings.

She selected a shopping cart with well-balanced wheels and pushed it toward the produce section. Her heels clicked along the concrete floor and echoed throughout the store as she headed for the brussel sprouts.

"G-good morning, Mrs. Jackson," Tariq hobbled toward Constance and, as usual, offered her the best pineapple he could find.

"Good morning, Tariq. Where's my hug?" Constance replied in her usual sing-song voice. She took the pineapple in one hand and extended her other gloved hand in Tariq's direction. She had read one time in a UCLA study that men and women needed eight to ten meaningful touches a day to maintain emotional and physical health. So, she made it a point to hug people.

Tariq smiled and looked down sheepishly as he limped a little closer to her. "Y-you look like you busy. Di-didn't think you'd have time today."

"Tariq Spencer, have I ever come in here and not hugged you?" Constance pinched his cheek.

"No, ma'am."

"All right then. Tell your mother I said hello and to call me about the church picnic."

"Y-yes, ma'am."

Constance placed the pineapple in front of her shopping cart and headed toward the dairy aisle. Tariq was right about one thing. She *did* have a lot on her mind. Her twenty-fifth wedding anniversary was at the end of the month. Where had the time gone?

It seemed like only a few months ago when she and Victor Senior had been planning a shotgun wedding—before either of them had finished their studies at Fisk. Three months later, she had miscarried.

The glimmer of what her life could have been flickered for a moment. But that ship had already sailed…along with all the hopes and dreams she'd packed up with her when she left east Texas for Nashville. She became the property of Victor Josiah Jackson and would be until the day she died.

Constance ran through her mental checklist of the items she needed for the rest of the week and proceeded to count the dinners on her fingers: spaghetti, enchilada casserole, fried chicken, and smothered pork chops.

Yes, all of Victor Junior's favorite meals were present and accounted for. If the checkout line wasn't too long, she might have just enough time to relax and read a bit before starting on dinner.

* * *

Later that afternoon, Victor Junior walked into the living room, and Constance could tell from his posture he had something on his mind. She hated when his shoulders stooped; it made him look like his father—big and shiftless.

"Stand up straight, Victor Junior," Constance insisted as she turned the page of the current issue of *Jet* magazine. She read the publication dutifully every week, as soon as it arrived in the mail.

"Ma, I got somethin' I need to tell you," he said.

"Do you mean you '*have* something' you need to tell me? 'Got' and using improper English ain't never got nobody nowhere." She looked over her black-framed glasses to make eye contact.

She knew it annoyed Victor Junior when she corrected his English. But that didn't matter. Constance put up with a lot of nonsense from her husband, and she wasn't about to take anything less than perfection from her son.

"Yes, ma'am," he sighed heavily. "I *have* something to tell you."

"What is it, dear? Come here and sit beside your mother." Constance patted the space on the settee next to her.

"Ma, first I want to say that I'm really sorry. I know you've worked hard to get me to college. And I really wanted to play basketball and move up North like you wanted. But things have changed...and I'm not going."

Constance slowly closed the magazine and placed it on the coffee table. She straightened her blue cotton housedress, folded her hands over her lap, and oriented her body so that Victor Junior's face was in full view.

"What do you mean 'things have changed'?" she repeated as she interlaced her fingers and gripped them together. Constance could feel the blood rushing to her head as she began to take short quick breaths.

He probably means that he just isn't going to North Carolina, prayed his mother. *He can't mean that he isn't going to college.*

"I'm not going to college. I'm..."

"Victor Josiah Jackson Junior, you *are* going to college. You are going to college. I have endured countless unspeakable acts from your father for the sole purpose of giving you a better life. And you will not throw it away. Am I making myself clear?"

Victor Junior stood up and placed his hands on his mother's shoulders. "Ma, it's not that I don't want to go. It's that Rachel's pregnant, and I'm gonna stay here and take care of her."

Constance let out a short shriek and then used her handkerchief to cover her mouth. Pressing her eyes together as tightly as she could, she began to think that this was a dream. This was all a dream, and in a few minutes she'd wake up and everything would be back to normal. But seconds later, Victor Junior was shaking her shoulders gently, trying to make her open her eyes.

"Look at me, Ma. Look at me. I'm sorry," he scrubbed his face with his hand and looked out the window. "I know how much you've sacrificed for me. But I won't be like *your husband*. I have to do right by Rachel and by my baby."

Constance sat in silence and gripped her handkerchief. She would not let Victor Junior see her cry. She was good at hiding her emotions. She just had to clear her head and think.

Maybe…just maybe…this child isn't his, Constance thought. *It could be someone else's. That Rachel is as fast as Jesse Owens. And there's no telling whose baby it could be. She'll have to get a paternity test. Yes, a paternity test. The baby's probably not his. Then life can go back to just as we've planned and hoped for.*

Deep down in the pit of her stomach, she knew the baby belonged to Victor Junior. But she wanted to hold onto the hope of college for him a little while longer. With that thought, a tear slid down her cheek. She wiped it and gently blew her nose.

"Ma, there's one more thing," Victor Junior hesitated.

Constance grew stiff. *What else could there possibly be? Victor Junior had just single-handedly repossessed every hope and dream she'd worked and prayed for, for the past 17 years. What else could there be?*

"Yes, Victor. What else is there?" she said clearing her throat.

"You see, Ma…I was wondering…if Rachel could stay with us?"

"Absolutely not," she huffed. "We've not even confirmed that the child is *your* offspring."

"The baby is mine," Victor Junior sent her a silencing glare. "It would just be for a while. She could use the extra bedroom. She can't stay with her parents, Ma. When Rachel told Pastor Andrews that she was pregnant, do you know what he did? He kicked her and spit on her. And I—I won't have her or my child living with someone like your husband. If you won't let Rachel stay here, then I'll leave too, and we'll find our own place." Victor Junior finished with more force in his voice than his mother had ever heard him use when speaking to her.

"Well then, Victor," Constance began in a slow measured tone. "It seems like you have everything all figured out, don't you? It seems to me, that *you* are making some very mature decisions for someone who was stupid enough to throw away his entire future on a floozy like Rachel Andrews. Just get out of my living room right now so I can think. I just need to think."

Constance flung her handkerchief onto the coffee table, and Victor Junior saw a vein begin to pop out of her right temple. That was a sure sign the grief had passed, and he knew he'd better leave her alone. She'd come around. She always did.

* * *

When Constance heard Victor Senior fumbling with his keys in the back door, she got up from her chair, flipped the kitchen light switch on, and crossed her arms. She'd been sitting there in the dark at the kitchen table since 10 p.m. trying to make sense of Victor Junior's revelation and contend with all the hopes and dreams that were slipping away.

She squinted as Victor Senior stumbled into her spotless kitchen and realized he embodied everything that had gone wrong in her life. His scraggly unshaven face. His stupid stutter. And that ever-present limp.

Victor Senior slammed the back door and gripped the side of the stove to remain on his feet. It was almost dawn, and his head was spinning from the loud music, hard liquor, and fast women he'd spent the last six hours with. Fortunately, his brain was also foggy— just the way he liked it.

Still, he was forced to shield his face from the maddening light and could feel Constance glaring at him, even though he wasn't able to look back. The sharpness of the light began to fade, and when it no longer seared his eyes, he could at least make out the frame of Constance's face. She owed her high cheekbones and silky black hair to her full-blooded Cherokee grandmother who had married a Negro slave.

And even in her house robe and after all these years, his wife was still a looker.

Victor took a deep breath and steadied himself. He hated Constance seeing him like this. He tried to tuck in his shirt tail and bring back some order to the white shirt that she'd washed and starched with such precision, but now looked crumpled and stained with red lipstick.

"Connie. Y-you waited up for me?"

"No, Victor," she answered with an air of superiority. "I abandoned waiting up for you many years ago."

Victor Senior could feel the chill in Constance's tone and noticed the arms crossed over her chest in judgment, not to mention her refusal to look at him. She didn't see him. She never had. He had loved her with his every breath, since the first day he saw her walking across the campus at Fisk University. But ever since she'd found out about Lucas and Mary Jane, she looked at him with a definite twinge of regret in her light brown eyes. A tear formed in his eye as he wondered, *Why can't we go back to the way things used to be?*

Big Vic took in two quick breaths to clear away the sadness and clenched his fist. In one giant limp, he was across the room and towering over her. Constance flinched to brace for the impact of what was coming, even as Big Vic grabbed a handful of silky locks and forced her to look him in the eyes.

"D-d-don't you *never* disrespect me again, Connie. *You hear me?*" Big Vic tightened his other large calloused hand around her throat.

Constance gasped for air and scratched at his wrists to try and loosen his grip. But all those years, moving boxes of flour at the Colonial Bakery, had made him strong as an ox.

She wasn't worried that he'd throw a punch, he hadn't beaten her for a while. The violence had come to a screeching halt a few years back when her screams woke up Victor Junior.

"Your son is not going to college," Constance choked as his grip tightened.

"Wh-what you mean, 'Junior ain't goin' to college?'" He loosened the hold on Constance's neck so he could hear her response.

"Your son impregnated my pastor's sixteen-year-old daughter," Constance pushed Big Vic's hand away and stood up from the table. "He's decided to decline the scholarship offer from North Carolina, go to work, and take care of them."

The news hit Big Vic like a freight train, and he slumped into the kitchen chair. He'd worked so hard to get Junior the tutors and the best schooling so his son could go to college. He hadn't even made him go to the country for the summer, but let him stay in town and study. He'd even bought him a green Buick after his sixteenth birthday—that way he could get back and forth to class and practice. *And this is how my son acts?*

For the past year, Big Vic had been bragging to the boys on the warehouse floor all about the scholarship offers and how his son was going to be a college man. Getting Victor Junior to college was the only thing that he and Constance had ever seen eye-to-eye. *How could he do this?*

Victor noticed that Constance was easing closer to the hallway. Probably trying to get away from him so she could get a few hours of shuteye before church started.

"Fix me some coffee," Big Vic sat at the table and rubbed his forehead. And just like he knew she would, Constance straightened her housecoat, turned back around, and headed toward the kitchen cabinet to pull out the coffee beans.

CHAPTER THREE

S haring prayer concerns was never to be confused with gossip. Not at Buchanan Street Missionary Baptist Church. On Tuesday evenings, the mothers of the church and the aspiring mothers of the church gathered to voice their prayer requests and then pray for the allotted time that was left.

Constance sat quietly at the far end of the circle, her legs crossed at the ankles. She adjusted her skirt several times and hadn't greeted the sisters with her usual cheek-to-cheek embrace and smile. She had nothing left to give. All she wanted tonight was some peace of mind.

Mother Jenkins began by sharing about her son's lost job. Sister Moss then shared her wayward husband was spending too much time with the deli girl at Cee Bee's. And when it came to Constance's turn, the room grew still. Everyone's eyes shifted toward her, and she gripped the bottom of her metal folding chair.

She needed to tell them. She needed help carrying the weight of Victor Junior's load. But the words wouldn't come.

So she sang.

It started with a quiet humming. Then she whispered, "Guide me, oh Thou great Jehovah. Pilgrims through this barren land." Sister Johnson scooted her chair close to Constance and wrapped her arm around her shoulder and joined in. Sister Bands stood.

"I am weak, but Thou art mighty." Sister Straight broke out her Martin Luther King, Jr. fan and waved it with fervor. One woman, who Constance didn't know, eased herself onto her knees on the bare concrete floor.

All the women joined in the plea. "Hold me with Thy powerful hand…" Each one sang. Their sound was strong, yet desperate—filled with the hope that someday all would be well, but with the reality that today was not that day.

When they ended their singing, they sat in the thick air and listened. Some rocked in their chairs. Some began to sing again. But all had tears. Constance took in a cleansing breath and swiped her cheeks. Sister Johnson handed her a Kleenex out of her oversized Bible bag.

Something felt different, and the knot that had been in her belly when she arrived was no longer there. Constance rolled her shoulders and shook her head from side to side. She had what she needed inside her. Her resolve was back, and she could endure whatever was to come.

Deacon Michael knocked on the door of the Warrior Room and opened it at the same time. He looked at his watch and then cleared his throat.

"Well, Sisters, it's a little before ten. Y'all plan on staying in here tonight?"

The sisters looked at each other puzzled and then let out a collective chuckle. Three and a half hours had passed, and no one had even thought about the time.

"No, Deacon Michael. We're a bit up in age for a lock-in. We got pills to take and beds to sleep in. We'll leave the overnighters to the young people." Sister Bands pulled herself back up to her chair and adjusted her wig.

The rest of the women smiled and nodded in agreement. It'd been too long since they'd had a prayer meeting like this. Constance felt lighter and judging from the faces of the other women, she knew they did too.

Victor Junior had shamed her by coverting with the pastor's daughter, but she wasn't giving up her church family for his foolhardiness. She was staying at Buchanan, and Pastor Andrews had better get used to the idea.

CHAPTER FOUR

B ig Vic was just as rigid as the schedule he kept. Every Monday morning at 7:30 he picked up and dropped off his work uniforms. He'd been working at the Colonial Bakery for the past 15 years and not long after he started he began to take his uniforms to the dry cleaners. Because the dough and flour had messed up Connie's washing machine. The guys at the plant had constantly ribbed him for that. And every now and again, one of the fellas would still say, "You don't make your woman wash your uniform?"

Big Vic never answered. The truth is, he always knew that Connie was too good to be washing his uniforms and clearly too good to be married to him.

He didn't deserve her.

Once again, the bell on the front door of McPherson's Cleaners clanged as he opened it. He dropped his uniforms on the counter, and Sally began with her usual small talk. He didn't know why Sally spent so much time jawing. Guess it was because she never married. Customers were the only people she saw, aside from her house full of critters.

A nice enough lady, she probably could've found a man if she fixed herself up some. But, her orange-ish blonde hair with black roots sticking through, and the smell of smoke that permanently wafted around her, and her teeth...God, her teeth could turn any man's stomach. Yeah, Sally really needed to fix herself up.

"Here's your clothes, Vic. The total's $16.25."

"Th-that's more than usual, Sally. What's the price change for?" Vic raised his eyebrow as he looked through his wallet for five more dollars.

"There was an additional surcharge. We had to wash your uniforms twice this time. They were extra dirty." Sally handed Big Vic a phone number scribbled on a napkin next to a kiss mark of red lipstick she'd found in his pocket.

"Uh-huh." Big Vic tried to escape Sally's glare, but the look on her face said it all—*You disgust me. How could Constance end up with a no-account man like you?*

Big Vic silently agreed. Constance had ended up with less than she deserved.

CHAPTER FIVE

B ic Vic never let his philandering ways interfere with his church-going. Without knowing it, he blamed his father. Years ago, his father had taken off with the oldest daughter of the family next door and never looked back. That made Victor Josiah Jackson the man of the house at the ripe old age of eight.

He existed to make his mother and three sisters laugh. And the laughs came easiest when he dressed in his mother's clothes and pretended to be her. It was the only time his mother's ever-present frown took a rest from her face. How Victor loved those women. And even now, once a year, to honor his mother's memory, he went home to Humboldt for the homecoming service at the church he grew up in.

Ebenezer Church of God in Christ, in Humboldt, Tennessee, sat one hundred yards from the railroad tracks and was suspended two feet above the ground by cement blocks. The dirt patch in front of the white clapboard building passed for a yard, and Victor could remember many Saturday afternoons when he was called on to rake it. He amused himself by using the rake as a paintbrush and the dirt as his canvas to create a world that only he noticed.

One of three country churches within five miles of each other along Route 31. The building held only a handful of people, most Sundays, who sat on the same pews they'd been sitting on since the early '40's.

Everyone knew that the plywood floor of the one-room church creaked every time someone thought about moving and the walls had needed a new coat of paint ten years ago—but the aging congregants just hadn't gotten around to it. As for the rest of the town, nothing much else had changed in this rural section of Tennessee in the last 50 years.

At Ebenezer's, Victor was just Radie's boy. He wasn't even sure if they knew his name. To them he was just Radie's son—the one who went off to war, was honored for bravery, became a Fisk-ite who married that pretty, light-skinned girl with the wavy hair, and bought a house in the big city.

The threat of having to pick acres and acres of cotton bolls from sunup to sundown, as far as the eye could see, was enough to make Victor hightail it to Nashville as soon as he finished high school. Thankfully, John Deere did most of the picking nowadays. But he would never forget how it was to work shares all day long in the sun, bend and pick as fast as he could, and all for $25 a week. The memory was tattooed forever. In his mind, working shares was akin to slavery, and he'd never heard of any picker clearing their debt and becoming a land owner.

No, he had left his cotton-picking days behind a long time ago. But he did come back once a year for his mama. Being there for homecoming always made her so proud. So he showed up, even after she'd passed on eight years ago. In some small way, it made him feel good to keep her memory alive.

As usual, the homecoming service had been too long. All Victor Senior really wanted to do was pass out a round of back slaps, give the mothers a few hugs, and get to eating. Meat wasn't as scarce as it had been when he was growing up, and he knew there'd be fried chicken, at least one ham, hog's head cheese, cornbread, beans, rice, and sweet potatoes. Still, none of it ever compared to the food he remembered being set out on his family's supper table after church on Sunday. His mama had been the best cook in the county.

Around noon, Victor Senior heard the pastor mention that he was "about to close"—the first time. So it'd be a while yet before the food was served. But a moment later, a new deacon stepped up to take a seat near the pulpit, and Victor Senior's heart began to race. He fumbled to get the inhaler out of his suit-jacket pocket. It was happening again.

The lights began to blink on and off in his head, and the beat of the closing drum made his heart pound faster. Big Vic shook his inhaler furiously and took a deep breath to help steady his heart.

The memories were creeping back—memories of his uncle, and try as he might, he couldn't erase them. Sweat stains began to show at his arm pits, and the hand towel he had brought along to church was soaked wet from constantly dabbing his forehead. He tried to maintain his composure while sitting on the hard, wooden pew and focus only on reading the pastor's lips.

Then he felt his throat tightening again even as he tried to force that hot August day from his memory. He needed to think about something else—the upcoming baseball season, Aunt Bernice's tea cakes she always made for Sunday dinner, the tiny black bird sitting in the rafters of the church sanctuary. But all he could think about was his uncle in the barn that summer 40 years ago.

Having received enough shouts to close, the pastor declared the doors of the church open, and Big Vic lumbered down to the altar. There, he quietly begged God to help him get rid of his immoral feelings.

"Please, Lord. Please. Help me," he tried to push back the memories. The nights he had spent away from Constance were not always with women but filled with dark juke joints and strange men. And the pain of not being in control of himself lingered.

He stumbled out of the church and headed toward his car parked near the railroad tracks. He didn't want to be that way anymore. He was a man, for God's sake, and he should be able to control himself. He pushed down his hunger and ignored the smell of peach cobbler trying to pull him back to the church. All he thought about were Connie and Victor Junior. They'd be better off without him. He wasn't even a man.

As Big Vic heard the blare of the train coming and the clang of the safety gate lowering, he remembered that day four years ago when he and Junior had fought. The look on Victor Junior's face was forever etched in his memory.

In a moment of sickness, he'd hit Connie. Junior heard her screaming and came running with his baseball bat. Big Vic couldn't bring himself to hit his son, so he didn't fight back when Victor Junior landed the blows with the Louisville Slugger. He'd gotten him that bat for Christmas, the year before. Their eyes connected for a split second—there was rage painted in his son's. He'd seen that look before, when he was in the war: survival mixed with fear.

Since that day, Junior had never looked him in the eye again, called him "Pops" or spoken his name. From that moment on, Big Vic was just "your husband" when Victor Junior spoke to Connie. If Big Vic came into the room, Junior left within seconds without a word.

He was a stranger in his own home, and he wasn't even a moral man. Connie and Junior deserved better.

They'd be better off without you, said the voice in his head.

Big Vic walked past his car and toward the coming train, repeating those same words to himself over and over again as he stepped onto the tracks and braced for the impact.

* * *

At Victor Senior's funeral, the pastor remembered him as a Korean War hero, a dedicated employee of the Colonial Bakery for 15 years, and a loyal husband.

Constance sat quietly and reflected on the Spring she and Victor met. He was so tall and handsome. All the girls had wanted to dance with him, despite the fact that he was just a freshman. Everyone knew about him.

Private Victor Jackson had charged up a hill under enemy fire to save a chaplain whose Jeep had been blown up. He had then carried the chaplain to safety and went back three times to help fellow soldiers. Eventually, Victor was wounded during the ordeal, but he'd saved four lives. Afterward, he was the first student to attend Fisk University on the G.I. Bill, and everyone on campus knew about his bravery.

On that night of homecoming in 1958, though, Victor had eyes only for Constance. She had felt him staring the entire evening, and after three of his requests, she agreed to a dance. He said he wanted to be her *only* dance partner for the rest of her life, Constance had believed him.

The next summer, they got married. And the next year, a short woman with two teenagers showed up on their doorstep. She said that the kids, Lucas and Mary Jane, were his, and he'd better start helping to pay their way. From that day on, Constance never looked at Victor the same.

Half her teacher's salary went to support those illegitimates, and she had never forgiven him for that. She let out a quiet sigh of relief as she glanced over at Lucas and Mary Jane, sitting three rows back. They'd come to stay one summer, but things were tense the entire time. Thankfully, they never returned.

Constance reached her gloved hand over to Victor Junior, patted him on the cheek, and gave him a weak smile. Things would be better for them now. For just the two of them.

CHAPTER SIX

A week after Victor Senior's funeral, Rachel came to live with what was left of the Jackson family. The house was dead silent except for the rhythmic creaking of Constance's rocking chair against the wooden floor. The steady sway helped to calm her nerves, and Constance needed all the calming she could get. She was waiting for the inevitable, gripping the arms of her chair until her knuckles turned white, and when she heard the front door opening, she willed herself to take a deep breath.

"Ma...Rachel's here," Victor Junior sat Rachel's cheerleading bag on the floor in the foyer, and the two teens—hell-bent on making adult decisions—peeked around the corner.

"Hi, Mrs. Jackson," Rachel looked down and tugged at the waist of her dress.

Constance gave her a once-over and made a mental note of how short the dress was. Their eyes met, and Constance decided not to comment—because they both knew the dress was too short to be appropriate. It simply confirmed the thoughts she already had about the girl—she was fast.

"Rachel, have a seat," Constance said through clenched teeth while nodding toward the settee, the crown jewel of her formal living room. Then without uttering a word, she oriented her steel gaze toward Victor Junior and commanded him to leave the room.

"Thank you so much for letting me stay here, Mrs. Jackson. Once my parents..."

"Is this even Victor Junior's baby?"

"What? Of course it's *his* baby. Why would you..."

"I have a paternity test scheduled for August when this baby is due. You can stay 'til then. But if this baby belongs to someone other than Victor Junior, you'll be on your own."

"This *is* Victor Junior's baby," Rachel said as her lip quivered, her eyes wide.

Constance glared at Rachel out of the corner of her eye and silently prayed to God that the little slut was lying.

Six months later, Sonny Josiah Jackson was born. After the positive paternity test, life fell into a rhythm for the next three years.

Victor Junior secured employment and worked weekdays as a call center representative for South Central Bell. It wasn't Constance's idea of a career path, but it paid the bills and came with health insurance. She did what she could to help Rachel finish high school—it simply wouldn't do for her grandson to have a high-school-dropout for a mother.

Constance settled into life with her makeshift family, but she could never shake the feeling that there should have been more.

CHAPTER SEVEN

On Sonny's third birthday, Constance's routine of normalcy came to a screeching halt—the day Victor Junior was murdered. One week later, Rachel turned the pillow over one more time. It was soaked through with her tears, and her head pounded from dehydration. She gave up trying to sleep away the memories, stumbled out of bed, and grabbed Constance's cordless phone from the dresser. She punched in the therapist's phone number she'd memorized.

"Hey Suzy, it's Rachel Andrews. How are you?" She pasted a smile on her voice and tried to sound upbeat. She hadn't seen Sonny in two days—she was just too tired to think of him.

"Doing fine, Rachel. Thanks for asking," Suzy paused and seemed to be searching for the right words. "Heard about what happened to Victor Junior from your parents on Sunday. Such a shame."

"Yeah," Rachel rested the phone on her shoulder, closed her eyes, and blew out three short breaths. That's how Dr. Hopkins had taught her to center herself. "Yeah, it's been a tough few days. I'm just trying to hold onto the little pieces of him that are left." Her voice cracked.

"Oh, Rachel. I'll be praying for you, sweetheart. I don't know why God let's these things happen. But I do know that all things work together for good."

"That's what they say, isn't it?" Rachel said through clenched teeth. "Look, Suzy, I need to get a new prescription called in. I lost my pills in the aftermath of everything."

"Sure, Rachel. I'd be happy to call in another one for you. What pharmacy do you prefer?"

"Haddox Pharmacy on Charlotte. Thanks," Rachel hung up the phone, and didn't bother waiting for a response. Suzy would come through. She always did.

Rachel collected her purse and lumbered down the steps to tell Constance she was going to the store to pick up a few items. Constance didn't ask any questions—she was probably relieved Rachel was leaving, even if only for a little while.

Within minutes, Rachel parked Victor Junior's mint green Buick in the handicapped spot in front of Haddox Pharmacy and glanced in the mirror to make sure she'd cleared away all the tear stains. Then she headed into the store to get some peace of mind.

She remembered the first time like it was yesterday. Rachel had been struggling with mood swings, and the school counselor recommended that her parents take her to see a therapist. The whole ordeal had been very hush-hush. What would people think if they knew that Pastor Andrew's daughter was being medicated for depression? Did the Andrews family not believe in "by His stripes we are healed?" That's what he taught the congregation, and a scandal would've erupted if the Andrews family were caught not walking the talk. So her parents came up with a plan.

Every two weeks, she would get out of school early for a "physical therapy" appointment for some made-up dance injury. Her mother had continued to insist that "physical therapy" was actually the truth, because "mental health" was really a part of "physical health."

Leaving the pharmacy, Rachel wrapped her scarf a little tighter around her neck.

I shouldn't be taking these pills, she thought. *Sonny does need me. Maybe I should get some real help.*

Rachel rushed into the payphone booth and shoved two quarters into the slot. And before she could change her mind, she dialed the number at the church office. Her dad picked up on the second ring.

"Good afternoon. Buchanan Baptist Church. Pastor Andrews speaking."

Rachel gripped the phone in both hands and held her breath. She hadn't heard her dad's voice in three years. Her mind went blank.

What should she say? What *could* she say?

Chapter Eight

Constance rested her head against the steering wheel and took in a deep breath as she stared at the manila-colored envelope that lay across her lap. Sergeant Walker hadn't made eye contact with her when he handed her the clipboard to sign. He had just cleared his throat and mumbled something about being sorry.

That's what everyone kept saying. Sorry.

She didn't want their sorrys. She just wanted to rewind the last four years and try to figure out where she had gone wrong. The margin for error had been so slim. She must have missed something along the way. She'd pushed too much. She'd asked for too much.

But what could she have done differently?

She'd gotten him into that school. She'd saved him from the perils of living a life without his father...she had stayed with Victor Senior for better or worse. She'd dragged her son to church until he'd grown big enough to resist. Constance had given him everything she'd had.

Still, he would never have the chance to fly.

His wings had been clipped, like so many other nameless statistics. But her son was supposed to be different. But he'd wound up just another ten-second news clip.

Constance turned the envelope over carefully and bit her lip as she broke the seal, then braced herself for what would be the last time Victor Junior would speak to her. Her hands shook as she took out his wallet and slowly opened it.

His driver's license. She traced the outline with her thumb. She remembered how she'd wanted him to wait to take his driver's exam until after his grades had improved. But Victor Senior, in an effort to get back into the good graces of his son, had taken him down to the Department of Motor Vehicles while Constance was at work—without so much as one lesson.

Next she found a picture of his face pasted to a South Central Bell employee badge—but it was not the student ID with a matching number that was issued to a college freshman.

Next—twenty-two dollars, the receipt for Sonny's cake, and a picture of Rachel in her cheerleading uniform.

Constance shook the remaining contents from the envelope into her lap, and out clinked Victor Junior's pocket change and the necklace and crucifix she'd given him on the day of his baptism. Victor Senior had joined her at church that day. She held the cross in the palm of her hand and wondered where her son was now.

She didn't have the strength to talk to God. He had taken her baby.

She closed her fist around the cross and exhaled all the feelings she'd choked down. Her shoulders quaked as she rocked back and forth. Her son was gone, and this was all she had left.

Chapter Nine

O ver the next year, Constance saw Sonny and Rachel less and less. Rachel moved into a Section-8 apartment a couple miles away, and at first, Constance had been relieved to see Rachel go. But then she missed seeing her grandson. He was her only link to Victor Junior now, and his smile reminded her of her own sweet son.

The last time Constance saw Sonny, though, his nose was running, his face was dirty, and he smelled like he hadn't been changed or bathed in days. Rachel, as usual, had been doing a poor job of caring for him. Even when Victor Junior was alive, that girl had never lifted a finger to care for her own flesh and blood.

Constance was attending Baptist Training Union Sunday afternoon when her belly began to knot and a sense of heaviness hung all around her. She crossed and uncrossed her legs, sat up straight in the hard pew, and tried to catch her breath.

She gasped as her memory flooded with all the moments she'd been unkind to Sonny. The time she'd smacked him when he spilled some apple juice on her freshly mopped kitchen floor, the morning she called him stupid because he couldn't remember to pull down his pants when he went to the potty, the evening she'd seen Rachel and Sonny at Victor Junior's gravesite and told them they were to blame for his death in the first place.

Constance had been evil toward Sonny since the day he was born. Now, she was reaping what she'd sown and was utterly alone in the world. Clenching the Martin Luther King, Jr. fan from the back of the pew in front of her, she began to fan herself, discreetly wiping away the moisture that had formed around her eyes.

Under her breath, she whispered a quiet prayer as the BTU lesson continued. "Lord, please give me a second chance with my grandson. Victor Junior is gone, and Sonny is the only chance I have to make things right. Forgive me for how I treated him. I was hurting. I just had so many hopes and dreams for my son. But if You give me a second chance, I'll do everything I can to raise him right. Amen."

Constance looked around the room and at the other six people in the class who tried to fight off the sleep caused by the monotony of Sister Caesar's voice. She inspected her nails and thought, *It's a shame a good Sunday afternoon had to be wasted sitting indoors.*

By the time the lesson was over, Constance had said a few more prayers—prayers that Sonny would remember her face and her name— and tried to figure out how to get him back into her life.

CHAPTER TEN

The blue lights flashed in Rachel's rearview mirror, and she looked over to Tito—her latest boyfriend—and noticed his body stiffen. She rubbed her hand across the back of her neck and slowed down to pull over in the parking lot of the Goodwill. She should've changed her license plate—she actually did have the new tags. As the officer approached the car, Tito emptied the content of his pockets onto the floor.

"Ma'am, are you aware that your license plate is expired?"

"Yes, officer. I've been meaning to change it. I've been really busy. I have…"

"License and registration please."

Rachel reached over to the glove compartment and hoped all the papers were there. But when she pulled on the latch, the first thing to fall out was Tito's 9 MM handgun. Rachel sighed, and her gaze met Tito's. The officer drew his gun and yelled, and Tito sent Rachel a silencing look.

Tito immediately put his hands on the back of his neck and interlaced his fingers, while the officer took a step or two back and continued to peer into the vehicle.

"Put your hands on the steering wheel, ma'am. Sir, get out of the car now and put your hands on the hood." Not taking his eyes away from the two, the officer pushed the receiver of the walk-talkie that sat on his shoulder and called for backup.

As Rachel placed her hands on the steering wheel, she looked at her reflection in the rearview mirror and noticed that while her hair was slightly tussled, her lip gloss still shimmered. If she was going to have her mug shot taken today, she was glad that, at least, she looked good.

The arresting officer read Rachel and Tito their Miranda Rights while other officers arrived to search the car. They discovered weed, unmarked pills, and...Sonny—asleep in the back seat. When a female officer arrived minutes later, she patted Rachel down to make sure she wasn't hiding any drugs or knives.

Sonny eventually woke up from his nap, and when he realized he was in the car alone, he began to whimper. Rachel looked at the female officer and motioned towards her cuffed hands behind her back.

"Could you un-cuff me for a minute, so I can pick up my boy?"

The female officer looked over at Sergeant Walker and with a look asked if it was okay. The sergeant shrugged, Rachel was un-cuffed, and Sonny was pulled from the back seat of the car.

"Quit making all that noise," she said as she wiped his nose. "There's nothing wrong with you."

"Ma'am, is there someone you'd like to call to come and pick up your child?"

"Nope, all we got is us."

"Okay then. Your child will be taken into youth services until your hearing. Are you sure there is no one you can call?"

Rachel let out a "tsk" and switched Sonny to her opposite hip. "Look, I already said it's just us. Call a social worker and get him in the system. He'll be better off there anyway."

The female officer raised her eyebrows and tried to assess whether or not Rachel understood her words or their implications. Judging from the fact that the young mother was wearing no shoes and seemed completely un-phased by the events of the last ten minutes, she concluded that she must be unwell.

"Okay, ma'am. Please hand me your child, and I'll place him in the back of the cruiser until someone arrives."

Rachel stuck Sonny out to the officer and then turned her wrists to Sergeant Walker to be cuffed again.

Just as Rachel was sitting down on the sidewalk, Sonny began to wriggle and then scream in the officer's arms. But Rachel wouldn't look at him, not even after he was shut into the back seat of the car.

"Mama! Ma-ma!" he cried over and over again and banged on the back window. Rachel stared at her hands and hoped no one she knew would see her sitting on the curb next to Tito.

* * *

Two days later, Constance walked into the lobby of the Cordell Hull Building and asked the security officer where to find the Department of Children's Services. From the sound of her sensible heels clicking across the floor, everyone within earshot knew she was there to conduct serious business.

Once the security officer signed her in, he directed her toward the second floor where Constance marched up to the receptionist and asked to see a Ms. Chantel Rickson.

"Do you have an appointment, ma'am?" the receptionist asked.

"No. I am a grandmother," retorted Constance, "and the last time I checked I didn't need an appointment for that. I'm here to collect my grandchild, Sonny Josiah Jackson, and I have no intention of waiting until y'all get around to setting an appointment," she finished her introduction without taking a breath.

"I see," the receptionist adjusted her eyeglasses. "Please have a seat," she nodded toward the waiting room, "and I'll see what I can do."

Constance took one look at the waiting room and instantly decided she would not be joining the crowd of despondent faces that'd been waiting there since God knew when. Getting Sonny back was the task at hand, and she was determined to do just that.

"No. I'll wait right here," Constance took a deep breath and willed herself to be larger. She adjusted the strap of the pocketbook on her wrist and continued to glare at the other woman.

With no other choice, the receptionist picked up the phone, covered her mouth, and whispered in hushed tones. But Constance didn't relax her glare.

She didn't smile.

She didn't nod.

She didn't move.

She did, however, apply the full force of silence and discomfort just as Reverend Lawson had taught in his non-violence training in the basement of Clark Memorial United Methodist. Those Tuesday night workshops had shaped her as a young Fisk-ite and more than once saved her from Victor Senior. The receptionist hung up the phone and cleared her throat, "Ms. Rickson will see you now. Your name, please?"

"Mrs. Jackson."

"Mrs. Jackson, please follow me this way. I'll show you to Ms. Rickson's office."

Constance allowed a slight grin to spread across her face as she fell in behind the receptionist. She "still had it." And she was relieved that she wouldn't be joining the waiting room full of relatives, friends, and whoever else was waiting to be reunited with their loved ones.

No, she was not going to sit in some dusty waiting room hoping for a chance to plead her case to get Sonny—someday. Sonny needed one thing right now, to be in a home with someone who loved him—and that someone was her.

The receptionist pointed in the direction of a bay of desks and to an office beyond where Constance could make out the shadow of someone's head appearing just above a stack of papers.

Ms. Rickson's office consisted of a desk covered with files and manila-colored folders piled in the corner, almost to the ceiling. A filing cabinet sat in the other corner, but it looked completely unused. Constance couldn't understand why Ms. Rickson failed to get the file folders *into* the cabinet. Her disorganization was probably the reason she had not returned the numerous phone calls, Constance thought. All that was past, though. She was here now—live and in living color—and she wasn't leaving until she got some answers.

"Mrs. Jackson, thank you for coming to see me. Please have a seat," offered Ms. Rickson without looking up from one of the files on her desk. "I see here that you are the next of kin for Sonny Jackson. Is that correct?"

"Do you see anyone else pushing their way in here to get to that boy?" Constance said as she raised one eyebrow and looked around the room for emphasis.

"No. No, ma'am, I guess you're right. Look, Mrs. Jackson. There are procedures to go through in order for me to release Sonny into your custody. There's family court, a site visit, the process of due diligence to ensure you are the only relative that will bring claims, and a whole bunch of other things."

"Let me ask you a question, Ms. Rickson," Constance looked at her dusty name plate on the desk. "What do you do?"

"Well, I'm a social worker," she said with a forced smile. "And I'm doing my best to improve society case by case."

"Yes, but what does that mean?"

"It means that I help individuals sort through the state child services system and solve problems that arise."

Constance let out an exaggerated exhale and reoriented her purse on her lap. "Yes, but somewhere in all that psycho-babble, aren't you supposed to be doing what's in the best interest of the child? Which in this case means, the best interest of my grandson, Sonny Josiah Jackson."

"Well, yes that's part of..."

"As far as I'm concerned, it's the only thing you do. And let me just take a minute and explain to you why I am in the best interest of Sonny. Then you can go ahead and do your job and award me custody. Because judging from all the bureaucratic red tape piling up on your desk," Constance tapped one of the manila-colored folders on the desk, "he's just a case-by-case basis to you. But, to me—*to me*—he is my only living flesh and blood."

"Let me ask you this—what factors do you take into consideration when looking for a foster parent?"

"Well...stability, education, home environment, and a number of other factors."

"Well, let's start with stability. I've lived in Nashville for the past 32 years. I've lived in my home over on Buchanan for 22 years. I've been a member of Buchanan Baptist Church for 30 years. And I am a graduate of Fisk University. Are you writing this down?" Constance asked as she let her gaze pierce Ms. Rickson.

"No. Not yet, just gimme a minute." She rummaged through her desk looking for a pen to write with, and then located Sonny's case file.

"Are you ready now?" Constance asked as she folded her arms across her chest. Ms. Rickson nodded for her to continue and then furiously began taking notes.

"Okay, we've already discussed stability and education. Now, let me explain to you the gravity of Sonny's need to be with me. He witnessed his father's murder at age three. He's spent the past year with his mother, Rachel—the sorriest excuse for a mother anyone could ever imagine. She has exposed him to drugs and alcohol, and no telling what kind of men have been running in and out of her apartment."

Ms. Rickson rubbed the palm of her hand as if she was getting a writing cramp. Constance gave her a look of mock pity and continued.

"The long and short of it is this, Ms. Rickson. You are charged with doing what's in the best interest of the child. I am in his best interest. He needs to be with me. I am his home and the only family he has. The alternative for him—for my sweet grandson—is that he ends up with some uneducated foster parent that this department *pays* to keep him."

Ms. Rickson stopped writing and looked up at Constance.

Constance seized the moment. "You know as well as I do, you have more work than you can handle. Sonny is a life. He is a life, and the best situation for him is to be with me. With me, he will be loved, and he will have a home—the same his father grew up in.

"Now, don't you want that for him, Ms. Rickson?" Constance then leaned back in her chair.

* * *

Three days later, Ms. Rickson showed up on Buchanan Street with Sonny in tow, explaining that Constance was being awarded custody of her grandson on a temporary basis, and that she would be back on a periodic basis to check in on him. Constance never heard from Ms. Rickson again.

It would be tough raising a four-year-old at her age, but Constance was no stranger to hard work. Life had prepared her for the handful that Sonny would be. All that mattered now was she had a second chance to get things right.

The next eight years felt like just a blip in time. Constance and Sonny filled their days with school, church, basketball, and food…and in that order. And the moments that Constance spent with her grandson kept Victor Junior alive in her memory. Sonny walked and talked just like his father. His temper, on the other hand, he inherited from both father and grandfather combined.

CHAPTER ELEVEN

C onstance and Sonny watched as the newest member of the congregation unwrapped her last baby gift. She and her husband had recently been transferred to Fort Campbell nearby, and the church ladies had banded together to make her feel welcome and help prepare for the little bundle of joy that would arrive in a week or two.

Constance tapped her grandson on the shoulder and motioned for him to follow her to the kitchen. "Let's start cleaning up," she said as she tried to suppress a yawn, "so we can get out of here."

Sonny picked up the broom from the corner and started sweeping the floor, while Constance wrapped and packed up the leftover food and loaded it into a cart. As she pushed it near the exit door, she called back to Sonny, "Go and get her car keys so we can load this food up for her."

"Yeah, Granny," Sonny sighed and thought, *Why can't you go and get the keys? You have two legs and two arms in good-working condition, just like I do.*

"Don't you mean, 'Yes, ma'am?'" Constance paused midstride to wait for his response.

"Yes, ma'am." He turned toward the fellowship hall and rolled his eyes, but not until his back was turned and he was out of striking distance. Then he navigated through the body of busy church ladies and asked for the keys.

"Y'all getting ready to load up the food?" Sister Bands pushed up her glasses and focused on Sonny.

"Yep."

"Help me up, boy. I need to get a to-go plate."

He reached down to help Sister Bands to her feet and then walked slowly as she hobbled along and leaned on him for support. They moved on in silence, and Sonny hoped he would never have to walk that slow when he got old.

"Sister Constance, come back here to get me a to-go plate before y'all take everything away." Sister Bands stood on her own two feet and made a sweeping motion toward the food, already packed and ready to go.

Constance gritted her teeth and forced a smile, "Well, we've already packed everything up…"

"Don't worry about it. Won't take me but a minute. Hand me a plate."

Constance looked in the cupboard, found a Styrofoam plate, and handed it to Sister Bands.

"Imma need more than one to-go plate, now, Sister Constance. You know, I got grandchildren."

Constance opened her mouth to say something and then thought better of it.

"Yes, Sister Bands. I'll give you *one* more."

As Sister Bands proceeded to shove in as much food as the two containers could handle, Constance glared daggers at her. What was left was barely enough to make a meal for the new military family.

That poor girl will have to cook for her husband this weekend after all, Constance thought, and she moved toward the cart and cleared her throat. Sister Bands got the message, finished up her pillaging, and headed back toward the fellowship hall on her own.

"I cannot *stand* people like that. Just plain greedy," Constance said through clenched teeth as Sonny helped her rewrap the food. "Let's just go." She gave the kitchen one last look—over, and satisfied that it was clean enough, turned off the light.

Pushing the cart toward the door, Sonny followed her to the parking lot where they transferred what was left of the food to the expectant mother's car, returned her keys, and then headed home in silence.

Constance needed the quiet to process her thoughts and come to terms with what was really bothering her. To begin with, she knew that Sister Bands hadn't even helped to pay for the shower. She was just a clinger-on and a last-minute invite. And then, she had the nerve to take a to-go plate!

Rude. And tacky. Something else was bothering Constance too. She'd seen this type of behavior in her students at school. A boy would fill his pockets with mints from her jar. A girl would threaten her best friend if she decided to be friends with anyone else. And then there was the constant fight over who got to be first in the lunch line. But it was so much worse when that type of behavior came from adults.

It was the difference between those who worried where their next meal was coming from and those who didn't.

"What you saw today, Sonny, was the perfect example of living like an orphan," she reached out to touch his forearm to make sure he was paying attention.

"Uh-huh."

"I mean it. That whole thing back there was about fear and taking care of me and mine without any regard for others. Sister Bands—she's a nice lady, but she is greedy as all get-out. And that greed comes from wondering where her provision comes from."

Sonny looked out the window and appeared to be half listening.

"Will you look at me for a minute?" Constance paused and waited for him to make eye contact. She switched her gaze between the road and checking Sonny's facial expressions to see if she was connecting.

"I never want you to be like one of those people that worries about whether or not they will be cared for, or where your next meal will come from. We've never been hungry, and we've never had to beg. Because He's always taken care of us," she pointed toward the roof of the car, "even in the tough times."

Sonny nodded dutifully and turned back to look out the window. Constance reached over and patted him on the knee.

He may not have grasped her words now, but it would all come back to him—someday.

CHAPTER TWELVE

T he afternoon school bell took forever to ring on the day of the roster announcements. Sonny had requested a hall pass during every single class period to go to the bathroom, just so he could see whether or not Coach Grimes had posted the roster early. He hadn't.

Constance was the one who had convinced him to try out. She said he would be a natural just like his dad. She'd lied. He couldn't dribble. His shoulders did something weird when he shot. And he didn't know the plays everyone else seemed to know...not to mention that he suffered with the notion of feeling naked every time he set foot on the basketball court.

You don't have what it takes to play ball.

"Why did I even try out?" Sonny said under his breath as he slugged toward the gymnasium to check the roster one last time. He didn't have what it took to be a ball player. The smallest and the slowest, he had only been to the neighborhood court a handful of times. Even there, he had always been picked last.

Finally. The end of the school day came. And as he approached the group of boys crowded around the roster, he tightened and fiddled with the straps on his backpack. Coach Grimes had told them that the roster would be posted at 2:45 pm, and apparently he had meant it. Because it had not been posted a second earlier.

Some exchanged smiles and dap, but no one gave him any indication of whether or not he would join the team or the group who had been cut.

The pit of his stomach felt empty as he braced himself for the worst. No matter what he saw on that list, he made up his mind to show no emotion, especially if he couldn't find his name. He raised his index finger and scanned the numbers...

1. Carlos Jenkins – Team Captain
2. Jonquis Taylor

3. Jontae Taylor …

…

13. Darryl Miller

14. Sonny Jackson

He took two steps back and tilted his head to refocus. He'd read his name on the team roster, and it felt fake. In a daze, he stepped away from the crowd and walked into the gym. It smelled of stale popcorn and sweat…and he liked it. The lights seemed brighter, and even the dingy floor seemed right.

He was part of this place now, and he would give it everything he had. Taking in a deep breath, he smiled as he looked at the scoreboard. One day those bulbs would light up for him and his number.

He took a final look at the bleachers and tried to imagine the energy on a game day. But that's when his mind drew a blank.…

Maybe he made a mistake. He turned to push open the heavy metal doors and checked the roster one last time.

Yep, his name was still there.

* * *

When not at church, Sonny spent most of his Saturday mornings walking around the neighborhood. Part of the reason was to see who was out, but the other part was to be seen. During the week, he had to wear a school uniform, but on the weekends, he got to wear his fresh white tees and starched jeans.

"Granny, I'm about to go out for a minute. You need something from the store?" Sonny leaned his ear against Constance's bedroom door.

"No, I don't need anything. Thank you for asking me, though. What time will you be home?" Constance called back.

"Later, Granny! I'll be back later, okay?" He opened the door and peered through to see how she looked. Her color was still a little off to-day, but at least she'd felt good enough to ask how long he would be gone.

"Alright, dear. See you later then." Constance buried her head in her comforter and sent up a silent prayer that the Good Lord would keep him safe for yet another day and bring him back to her. Whenever he left, she feared something might happen to him.

She knew it was wrong. She should have been more trusting. But life had taught her to pray for the best and prepare for the worst.

* * *

Sonny bounded down the front steps of the house and set out to see what this Saturday had in store. Maybe he'd play ball, or dice, or head to the Rivergate Skating Rink. That was the best thing about Saturdays— you never quite knew what was going to happen.

Just as Sonny turned the corner, he ran into Jonquis and Jontae Taylor. Supposedly, they were twins...but looked nothing alike. They did have one thing in common, though; both had beef with Sonny.

Sonny's heart sank into his stomach and he tried to maintain eye contact. He would not under any circumstance show that he was scared.

The twins started circling like vultures.

"You clean today, ain't you, Sonny?" said Jontae.

"Yeah. Fresh to death," Jonquis sniffed.

They stood on either side of Sonny, their breath smelling like hot dogs and corn chips, as they whispered threats in his ears. "You think you so smooth with those new J's, don't you?" Jontae said. "Well... they'll look good on Jonquis and you gonna be out here on the sidewalk with just socks."

The blood rushed to Sonny's ears as he clenched his fist and gritted his teeth. He wasn't about to give the twins his brand-new Air Jordans. No matter what. He liked the way he felt in them. And last evening, it seemed like more girls smiled at him—that made him feel a little taller and a little stronger. His granny had had the shoebox on his bed when he got home from school yesterday. *Why did he have to run into the twins?*

Jonquis chimed in, "They look just my fit too. What size them shoes?" Sonny looked straight ahead. His mind was spinning, searching for the right words to say, to get himself out of this. Meanwhile, Jonquis moved just close enough that his chest rubbed against Sonny's shoulder for emphasis. Then he forced out a little chuckle as he lined up his foot next to Sonny's to judge his shoe size.

"Don't answer that, Sonny," a voice said.

Carlos Jenkins had walked up behind them without making a sound and reached over to give Sonny dap. He crossed his arms over his chest and gave the twins a nod. Relieved to see someone he knew, Sonny let out a little grin and let his head fall back. Carlos was, actually, someone everyone out north knew.

Before middle school, Sonny had seen Carlos play ball at the YMCA in the 10-and-under group, but Carlos was too good for rec center ball. He'd moved up to AAU and also played on the school team. He was taller and bigger than everyone else on the court. No doubt, he would be going to the draft straight out of high school.

Carlos saved Sonny from a beat-down and a loss of pride that day. And with that act, he bought Sonny's loyalty.

CHAPTER THIRTEEN

Sonny stared at the cracks in the ceiling of Carlos' room and tried to clear his mind of the movies they'd watched before bed. After it was over, he'd wedged his sleeping bag as close to the wall as possible and stared wide-eyed until his sight adjusted to the darkness.

But he still couldn't force the image of the red-haired doll with the stiches across her face from his mind. The night sounds in Carlos's apartment didn't make things any better. Sonny wanted to go home. But he would have to wait until morning. Carlos would never stop roasting him, if he left scared in the middle of the night because of those movies.

Carlos' mother had dropped off the two Blockbuster tapes, pizza, and told them she'd be down the street at a neighbor's house. It was past 2 a.m., and she hadn't come home yet.

Sonny shut his eyes and tried to imagine that he was at home in his own bed, with Constance just down the stairs waiting for him to fall asleep. She would come up in a few minutes, pull her rocking chair close, and pray for him once she thought he was asleep.

A few hours later, Sonny woke up to see the sun beginning to peak through the crack in the plastic blinds. Morning. He could finally go home. He unzipped his sleeping bag and looked over at Carlos. He was still knocked out.

Sonny started to wiggle out of his sleeping bag, but he froze in horror. He reached down to pat his shorts and then his sleeping bag. Both were soaked. His thoughts raced as he tried to figure out how to get of there and back to safety with his Granny.

Carlos would roast him for days if he found out that he had wet the bed. He just had to get back to Constance. That was the only thing that would save him. He tip toed to the kitchen and found a stash of plastic bags. He rolled up his sleeping bag and stuffed it inside. Then he slipped his gray jogging pants over the top of his night shorts.

He'd shower and change when he got home. He found his shoes next to the stairway, slid his feet into them, and crept toward the front door. Carlos hadn't moved an inch, and no telling where his mother was. Sonny undid the security chain and opened the door slowly. It creaked loud enough to wake the dead, but it didn't seem to bother Carlos.

Outside on the sidewalk, Sonny took in a deep breath and tried to steady his legs that felt like jelly. He'd escaped, and Carlos wouldn't know a thing.

* * *

Constance sat at the kitchen table when Sonny unlocked the back door with the key that hung around his neck.

"What are you doing home so early?" She lifted a cup of tea to her mouth and waited for him to respond.

"Didn't sleep good last night. Just wanted to come home."

"Why didn't you sleep *well?*" Constance emphasized the word "well" and gave Sonny a knowing nod.

Sonny stood in the middle of the kitchen, holding the grocery bag containing his wet sleeping bag, in front of him. *Should I tell her the truth? Or just leave it?*

Don't tell her.

Tell the truth.

"Promise you won't get mad?"

"I never get *mad.* A *mad* person is someone who's insane and out of control. I have every use of my faculties, young man." Constance tapped herself on the forehead and continued. "Now, I just might get *angry* now and then. Especially, if you are doing something that you ain't got no business doin'. If that's the case, then I have every right to be angry. But even when I *do* get angry, I never lose control."

Sonny gripped the edge of the table and looked down at the red and white linoleum that covered the kitchen floor. "Watched some scary movies with Carlos last night and wet the bed."

Constance moved closer to Sonny and held his chin in her hand. "Look at me, Sonny." He peeled his eyes up from the table slowly and tried to blink back the tears.

"Sit down here beside me," she moved the kitchen chair back from the table, and Sonny sat his bag down. Constance wrapped her arms around his shoulders and leaned her head against him. She said a silent prayer as she tried to figure out what to say.

More than anything, in this moment, Sonny needed to know that he was loved. But he also needed to know that his decisions held consequences. *Give me wisdom, Lord, I don't want to wound him while he's hurting.*

Constance opened her eyes and positioned her chair to face Sonny. "First, let me say I'm not angry with you, dear. You made a decision, and there were consequences. But more than anything, I'm sad. Sad, because I never want to see you hurting or afraid," her voice broke.

"I've done everything I know to do. You are getting older now, and you're gonna have to make mature decisions about where you go, what you watch, and who you listen to. Because it's gonna affect your peace in here," she tapped her finger on his heart and waited for him to respond.

"I know, Granny. I know. I just…"

"Son, it's one thing to know. But it is a whole 'nother thing to do. I'm not always gonna be around to protect you and tell you what do. You're gonna have to know how to hear God. I *know* that He talks to you, but you just don't listen."

Sonny picked at his lips and stared at the table.

A thought crossed her mind—*he needs to know you love him.*

"You know I love you, right?" Constance sighed.

"Yeah."

"Okay. Go put your stuff in the laundry room and get yourself cleaned up. Let's make you a good breakfast and get this Saturday started off right," Constance ran her hand through his dark curls and tickled his chin.

Sonny pushed her hand away and smiled, "Stop that, Granny."

"Boy, you might be bigger than me, but you still not too big to get tickled. I'm stronger than I look," she pulled up the arm of her house-coat to show him the definition on her arm.

"Okay, Granny. Okay." He got up from the table and leaned over to kiss Constance on the cheek. "Be back in a few minutes. Don't start breakfast without me."

* * *

When Sonny returned to the kitchen several minutes later, Constance got up from the kitchen table and placed her Bible on the top of the refrigerator.

"What would you like for breakfast?"

"Bacon, eggs, and hash browns."

"Okay, then get my cast iron skillet. I'll start chopping up the potatoes."

The smell of bacon and onions began to fill the kitchen as the meat and hash browns started to sizzle. Grandmother and son stood side by side in front of the stove.

Constance looked over at Sonny and thought about the time she used to spend in the kitchen with Victor Junior. He was a good cook too—just like her—and loved to eat his own food. She wondered if she would ever stop missing him. She wrapped her arm around Sonny's waist and thanked God that at least she had a piece of her son with her.

Sonny leaned down and hugged Constance back, then used his free hand to pull up his pants.

"Where is your belt, young man?"

"Ugh. Come on, Granny. Not now."

"What do you mean 'not now'? You saw fit to get dressed but leave a vital part of your clothing upstairs?"

"Granny, we just chillin'."

"Doesn't matter. It's the principle. Gentlemen wear belts. I'm raising a gentleman. Not a hooligan," Constance waved her spatula for emphasis.

"Okay. Okay. I'll get a belt."

"Thank you."

"Can I do it after breakfast?"

Constance tilted her head to the side and looked at him as if he was crazy.

Sonny shook his head and turned to head up the stairs.

CHAPTER FOURTEEN

Sitting on the edge of the bench in the locker room, Sonny covered his head with a towel. He just needed to block out the world. Block out the last four seconds of the game. And figure out what would be his next move. His sweat mixed in with his tears, as he tried to get the courage to face his teammates.

"You never should-a been on this team anyway," Jontae shoved Sonny in the head as he walked by to get to his locker.

Sonny tried to ignore him as he re-ran the play in his head. The other team had inbounded, and he'd stolen the ball from their starting guard. His shoes squeaked as he pivoted, took two steps, and used the power in his legs to fire off one last shot before the buzzer.

He clenched his eyes shut and waited to hear from the crowd—whether or not it was good. Cheers. Then an eruption of laughter. When he opened his eyes, everyone was laughing and pointing at him. Constance included. He'd scored a winning three-pointer...for the other team.

Sonny rubbed his face with the towel and stood up. He couldn't hide anymore, so he might as well get it over with. Inside the locker room, the team seemed to be going about their business, except for Jonquis and Jontae. Both stood in the corner talking and nodding in Sonny's direction. He opened his locker and got his stuff to change clothes and then paused as Jonquis stepped over to him.

"You need to go 'head and quit the team."

"I'm not quitting, okay," Sonny shifted his weight right to move around Jonquis and head for the showers. Jonquis grabbed his arm.

"I'm not done with you."

Sonny jerked his arm away and threw down his towel and clothes on the bench.

"I already told you, I'm not quitting. So you need to step."

"Step? What?" Jonquis took off his jersey in one strong motion and stood nose-to-nose with Sonny. "You want it with me then, Sonny? Let's go. I been waitin' long to give you this whuppin'. You light-skins need to be taught a lesson."

Sonny's jaw flexed as he took a deep breath and peered into the whites of Jonquis' eyes. He knew as soon as he struck Jonquis, his brother Jontae would jump in. The twins were known for double-teaming and had never seen a fight that was fair.

"What you waitin' for? I thought you was hard," he took his index finger and shoved Sonny in the forehead.

Sonny took a step back. And then the camel's back broke. He grabbed the chair in the corner of the locker room and hurled it at Jonquis, missing his target but smashing the chair into the wall. Sonny barreled full-force into Jonquis and pinned him against the wall, gripping his neck with his right hand and wailing on him with his left.

Let him go.

No…he deserves this!

Jontae jumped in and tried to grab Sonny around his neck, but Sonny managed to also dot his left eye in between blows to Jonquis' face. The team froze in place as they watched his rage erupted into lava.

Coach Grimes, just next door, must have heard the ruckus and came charging into the locker room. He grabbed Sonny's free hand with both fists, and the fog lifted.

"What are you doin', boy? Are you crazy!?"

Sonny stared at Coach Grimes with a dazed look. Then he rubbed his chest with his free hand. "I don't know what happened, Coach. The twins was popping off at the mouth, and I just…"

"Go to my office," Coach Grimes raised his hand in a silencing motion and then pointed toward the door. "Taylors—clean yourselves up and get out of here. I'll deal with y'all later."

"But Coach, you saw what he did."

"Whatever he was doin' was provoked by whatever you two did first," Coach Grimes towered over the twins and rested his clenched fists on his waist.

Still mumbling underneath their breath, the twins gathered their things and headed toward the showers.

"The rest of you, get this locker room cleaned up. Can't believe y'all stood there like some dummies and watched your teammates fight. What have I told y'all about team unity?" Coach Grimes found it hard not to yell even louder as he made eye contact with each of the boys on the team. Then he headed toward the door, but stopped short. "And another thing—the first one to mention *that shot*, or any of this again, is off the team."

The boys nodded in understanding and tried to avoid looking at him. Coach threw open the locker room door and stormed toward his office to handle Sonny. But thought better of it and took a lap around the school first—to cool down a few degrees.

When Coach stepped into his office 15 minutes later, Sonny was sitting in the chair across from his desk, biting his nails. Bowing his own head, he strode across the room, sat down, and took a deep breath.

The silence sang as Coach Grimes tried to figure out what to say to the boy. The only reason he'd agreed to coach the sixth-grade team in the first place was because Constance had made him promise that he'd keep an eye on her grandson. Now this boy was wilding out. He cleared his throat and paused another few seconds.

"Son, you have got to get control of your anger..."

"Look, the twins started it, and I was not about to..."

"I'm not talking about the twins, Sonny," he leaned across his desk and rested his chin on his fists. "Leave them to me. What I'm talking about is that blind rage I saw back there. What happened to you in that locker room?"

Sonny straightened his shirt and tried to focus on the Adidas strips on his basketball shoes. "I don't know, Coach. Jonquis tried to punk me, and I just snapped."

Coach Grimes let out a sigh and rubbed his shiny head. "You have got to get control of your anger. No matter what anyone else does, *you* control how *you* respond," he tapped his knuckles on the top of his desk, and Sonny looked up to meet his gaze.

"You could have left the gym today with a criminal record and been expelled from school. What would that have done to your grandmother?"

Sonny looked at the National Championship ring on Coach Grimes' finger and shrugged.

"It would have killed her, that's what! ... But I get it. I had the same problem. I almost stabbed a classmate with a pair of scissors because he waved a confederate flag in my face." He paused as he thought about what his life would have been like had he had better aim back then. "But I grew up and learned that I couldn't give my power away. I couldn't let someone else write *my* story based on how I responded to their actions. You have to take responsibility for your choices. Told your dad the *exact* same thing 12 years ago, but he didn't listen. I had to be stronger, and so do you, son."

"Am I off the team?"

"No," Coach Grimes shook his head and wondered if Sonny had picked up anything he'd just said. "As far as I can tell, they both jumped you, and you had the right to defend yourself."

Sonny nodded in agreement and collapsed further back into his chair.

"But you're not getting off scot-free. I want you to write out every verse in Proverbs that deals with anger—and write each verse ten times. You can give it to me at the next practice. Maybe you'll learn something."

"Okay, Coach."

"Now get out of here. Your grandmother's waiting for you."

Sonny gathered his things and hustled out the door, forgetting to say thanks.

Coach Grimes interlaced his fingers behind his head and leaned back in his chair. His gaze fell on the picture of the National Championship Team he'd coach in 1985. Victor Junior had been the starting point guard and had led his team well in his last year of basketball. Coach Grimes hoped he could return the favor by keeping his son on the straight and narrow.

CHAPTER FIFTEEN

The next morning, the sun beamed past the burgundy curtains which Constance had pulled back against the kitchen window. She could hear the chirp of the willows while they ate at her apple-colored bird feeder. She'd made Sonny an egg and cheese omelet, hash browns, and pork bacon. Although Constance hated the smell of pork (from all those years of seeing pigs slaughtered in Wharton), she knew it was Sonny's favorite, and she wanted today to be a special day.

Sonny came down for breakfast with sleep still pasted to the corner of his eyes. He shuffled over to Constance and gave her a kiss on the cheek. He knew she always made pork bacon when she wanted to cheer him up.

"Sonny, I want to give you something," Constance said as she retrieved a little wooden box from one of the kitchen cabinets. "Go ahead and sit down." He probably had seen the box many times. But this morning, his grandmother was pushing it toward him.

"What is it, Granny?"

"Open it up and see, honey," she said as she ruffled his hair. He was 13 now and looking more and more like Victor Junior every day. How she missed her son.

Sonny sat up straight and wiped his hands on his pajama pants. Then he opened the box slowly and peeked inside. There laid a little gold cross on a golden rope chain and a picture of his dad and his mom watching him blow out the candles on his third birthday cake.

It was strange to see the picture. Sonny had forgotten what his dad's face looked like. Sometimes, he thought he'd seen him in a crowded place or walking through the mall. But whenever he caught up to that particular man, he looked nothing like the dad he faintly remembered.

Sonny held the small frame in his hand. He kept staring at his father, as if waiting for him to say something. There in the picture, his dad was smiling at him with his hand on his shoulder, waiting for him to blow out the candles. He wasn't looking back at his dad though. He was looking at the fire dancing on the candles.

Constance, cleared her throat, despite not wanting to ruin the moment. She noticed Sonny holding his breath and trying to capture the feeling in the photograph.

But she needed him to know something. "Your father loved you dearly," she said softly. "I wanted to give this to you on your 13th birthday, so even after I'm long gone, you would always know."

Sonny looked up at Constance and nodded slowly. His grandmother had cleared the house of any sign of Victor Junior after his death and explained over and over again to Sonny that she had just wanted to forget the pain.

But today, *today*, Sonny got to remember and crawl back to a happier time, when his dad and Rachel were sitting next to him, sharing a cake with him, and celebrating. A time when he was the center of their world.

"The necklace was your grandfather's and then your father's. I'm not sure where Victor Senior got it, but I thought you should have it," Constance continued. Sonny was still staring at the picture of his dad and still trying to grasp what that moment had actually felt like.

"Sonny, listen to me for a minute," Constance said as she placed her hand on his shoulder. "In our land of origin—Africa—there were many rites of passage based on your tribe. The rites marked the importance of passing from one stage of life to the next and outlined your responsibility to the community."

Sonny looked up at Constance quietly. She had never spoken to him before as if they were equals, and it was awkward to hear.

"Sonny, you and I don't have much of a community now. Our family consists of you and me. But I'm giving you these gifts today because I want you to know that no matter what happens, you have been loved. Deeply and completely."

He sat there in silence, his eyes still glued to his dad's face and his heart wishing he could hear his dad say his name just once.

* * *

Constance had meant that day to mark his transition to manhood. Sonny was 13 now, and she couldn't treat him like a boy anymore. But it felt like something else was happening. Over the next few months, Sonny came home less and less for dinner. He said he wasn't hungry. Or he was at school late. Or he was practicing ball. But Constance knew the truth—she could feel it in the shadows.

CHAPTER SIXTEEN

Young's Market was the closest thing to a grocery store in the Casey Neighborhood. Most of the canned goods were dented, and there was never any fresh produce. But the neighborhood put up with the business anyway, because the Korean owner took stamps and sometimes dropped in an extra couple of fortune cookies.

Each corner of his store was crammed with as many packaged goods as the shelves could hold. The Tide detergent sat next to the Oodles of Noodles, and the Oodles of Noodles was stacked next to the frozen food chest. All four aisles were always packed to capacity. And everyone knew that Mr. Young never missed a day of sweeping or mopping, but the grime always returned within a few hours...carried in on the shoes of the locals.

One afternoon, when he should have been in school, Carlos wandered into the market and nodded at Mr. Young. Sonny shuffled close behind. But he was so focused on avoiding eye contact with anyone, that his shoulder knocked over the broom leaning against the front wall. Carlos shot him a glare as he wrestled to make the broom balance again.

Don't do this.

The boys began to hunt up and down the aisles until they found what they were looking for—the Oreos. Sonny kept swallowing hard and staring down at his feet.

"Get over hear, dude," Carlos said in a hushed whisper.

Sonny stepped over and bent down like he was looking at something on the bottom shelf while Carlos angled his body to block the reflective mirror. In one swoop, Carlos shoved the package of Oreos under his sweatshirt.

Sonny stood straight up as if he had been given an electric shock. He just wasn't good at boosting. Carlos sighed.

"Go get the gum, dummy."

"Oh. Okay."

Heading to the register, Sonny picked up the first pack of gum he laid his hands on and handed it to Mr. Young, who rang up the purchase of 27 cents. He let his gaze fall on Sonny for a minute but didn't say anything.

Mr. Young waited for the receipt to print, handed it to Sonny, and asked, "How's your grandmother doing?"

Sonny cleared his throat, mentally begging it not to crack.

"She doin' fine, Mr. Young. Good. Really good."

Sonny shoved the change and receipt into his pocket.

"I'll tell her I saw you when I at church next time," offered Mr. Young. "Your grandmother such nice lady." He let his gaze fall and then paused a few seconds to let the silence sink in. "Good Christian lady...who taught you better than stealing," he pointed at Sonny's chest.

"Wh-What? Wha-d'ya mean?"

"I know you and boy took Oreos. But because your grandmother is good lady, I will let go if you empty trash in back of store."

Sonny didn't know how to respond. So he just made his way back over to Carlos as if he was being held at gunpoint.

"Carlos," he whispered, "Mr. Young knows about the Oreos. He says he'll let it go if we take out the trash."

"Pshhh," Carlos let out a long wind, grabbed Sonny's collar, and grumbled through his teeth. "Dang, Sonny. If you weren't acting so scared, we could-a been out-a here."

Sonny shrugged.

"Tell 'em we'll take out the trash."

Relieved that Carlos had agreed, Sonny felt his shoulders loosen as he headed back toward the checkout counter.

"We'll take out the trash, Mr. Young. Just tell us what to do," Sonny said looking down, tracing the crack of the cement floor with his red and gray Jordans.

"Trash is bagged. Just go to back, get bags, and put in dumpster down the alley. You can use back gate."

Carlos and Sonny headed to the back room. The TV/VCR combo blaring a Korean soap opera dimly lit the room. Mr. Young's daughter, who did the inventory, glanced up from her perch on a milk crate and gave them a "What-are-you-doin'-here?" look.

"We're here to take out the trash," Sonny quickly explained.

The daughter pointed to the corner, shrugged, and sat back down. Sonny noticed that she was really pretty, except for the pimples on her forehead, with waist-length, jet-black hair. If he hadn't been in a hurry to get out of the store and get this over with, he might've stayed to conversate.

The back room was dark and smelled of rotten eggs and metal. Sonny guessed the bags were full of spoiled food, and he was not looking forward to getting his clothes and shoes dirty. But it was better than his granny finding out what he had done.

She hadn't been feeling well lately, and he knew something like this would hurt her. So, he rolled up his sleeves, looked at the bags piled almost to the ceiling, and sighed. *Let's just get this over with.*

But Carlos had a different plan. He had been standing back with his arms crossed over his chest, also sizing up the 30 or so bags of garbage. "Mahn. I ain't about to take out all this trash," said Carlos as he nodded toward the door. "Let's bounce."

"Wh-what?" Sonny's heart skipped a beat. He couldn't believe that Carlos still wanted to skip out after they had been caught. "Nah, man. Just come on. It won't take long."

Carlos wasn't listening. He tapped Sonny on the shoulder and headed toward the slightly opened back door. Sonny stood there as if his feet were stuck to the pavement. If he didn't go, Carlos would be mad, and he'd be on his own again. If he did go, Granny would know what he and Carlos had been up to. He rubbed his forehead. He couldn't believe that Carlos was doing this *again.*

Just then, Carlos came back and half-dragged Sonny out the back of the store by his collar. "Don't forget—you *owe* me," Carlos said with a knowing grin.

He's right.

Sonny did owe Carlos. He didn't have to worry about what side of the street he walked on anymore. He didn't have to worry about who spoke to him and who didn't. Everyone knew he was with Carlos. And that was protection.

Sonny barely had time to put back the trash bag he had been holding. As Carlos continued to push him, he tried to shake the guilt that settled in around him, but it wouldn't lift.

The next week Sonny got a little relief, because Carlos finally decided to give up on skipping school. He got tired of trying to find food every day that he was out on his own. And an empty stomach helped him to remember the three meals he ate each day, courtesy of school breakfast and lunch tickets and the afternoon tutoring program at the church down the street.

CHAPTER SEVENTEEN

Constance hadn't forgotten about the shoplifting stunt Sonny had pulled a few months ago with Carlos. So she went against her better judgment and decided to "incentivize" his educational performance. She'd been thinking about it all summer. It just didn't seem right to pay a child for making good grades. Victor Junior had made good grades because she told him that he had better. But things were different with Sonny.

Constance handed Sonny the last plate to dry and put away. She let the soapy water drain out of the sink as she thought about the ground she was giving up. Just didn't seem right, but Constance couldn't think of a better plan. He put away the last dish, and she dried her hands on the kitchen towel.

"Would you like a bowl of ice cream?" Constance made eye contact with Sonny, and she knew why he let out a sigh. "Don't worry, I'll wash the rest of the dishes when we're done," she said with a knowing smile. It was a strict rule in the Constance Jackson household that every dish be dried, washed, and put away before bedtime.

Sonny nodded and got two bowls from the cabinet and two spoons from the drawer. While Constance dished out two scoops for him and sat down.

"Eighth grade starts next week, and this year is going to be different."

Sonny didn't look up from his bowl.

"I mean it," Constance tapped her finger on the table for emphasis. "That foolishness you and that boy pulled could've sent you in a different direction. You are going places, Sonny...if you don't let Carlos..."

"If I don't let Carlos what? Granny, you don't know half the stuff he do for me."

Constance mentally ordered herself to stay calm as she stared at the flower pattern on the tablecloth. If Victor Junior had ever spoken to her like that, it would have been the last time he spoke.

Just stay focused.

Constance looked toward the ceiling and took a deep breath, "Here's what I propose. For every report card you bring home with only A and B marks, I'll take you and that boy out somewhere nice."

Sonny lowered his head to read Constance's face. She couldn't be serious.

"But your friend can't go if he fails any of his classes. I simply will not reward failure." Constance held Sonny's gaze for a few seconds and then stood to return the ice cream to the freezer.

Sonny shoved the last two spoons of ice cream in his mouth and placed his bowl in the sink with a clang.

"Thanks, Granny," he leaned down to kiss Constance on the cheek. Constance held him close for a split second and took a deep breath. Perhaps she hadn't made a deal with the devil.

"Night," he turned and headed toward the stairs.

"Don't forget to say your prayers."

"I won't, Granny."

She'd been saying the exact same phrase, ever since he was in the fourth grade when he'd asked her to stop tucking him in. Sometimes Sonny said his prayers, and sometimes he didn't. Either way he always promised that he wouldn't forget.

CHAPTER EIGHTEEN

Sonny decided to drag the heavy hospital chair over to Constance lying in the bed. She was hooked up to all kinds of wires and tubes, and he just wanted to be closer to her. The nurse stared at the red flashing numbers displayed on the machines and made a few more notes on her clipboard.

"Please don't knock anything over, okay?" she said without looking up from her papers.

"Yeah, okay."

Coach Grimes nodded an okay as well, and placing his hand on Sonny's shoulder, he added, "Let me help you with that, Son."

"Thanks." Sonny stood next to his sleeping grandmother while Coach Grimes rearranged the furniture, and after Coach left the room, Sonny took her limp hand in his and tried not to think about what life would be like without her. She was everything he had, and he could not imagine what would happen to him if she left.

"Granny, please get better. I promise I'll act right if you just come back," Sonny lowered his voice to a whisper as he rested his forehead on hers. Although she was still breathing and the nurse had said she'd recover, he couldn't shake the feeling that he was already alone in the world.

A faint memory started to take shape, and it felt like he'd been in this moment before. Or he had at least seen it in his mind. It was a split second, and it was just one image. But being here felt familiar.

The beeping from her heart monitor brought him back to the present, and the memory faded. Sonny pulled the blanket up to his grandmother's chin. He knew she hated to be cold, and a tear rolled down his cheek.

Turning the TV off, he decided to curl up in the chair next to her bed and then stared at her motionless face until he fell asleep.

Coach Grimes came back to the room after talking to the doctor and used another blanket to cover Sonny up. He could see they were both tired and just needed to rest. But he was determined to be there, ready and waiting, when both grandmother and grandson woke up.

* * *

Constance was the first to wake up the next morning and to a hospital room full of flowers and cards. Sonny was still sleeping, cramped in the chair beside her bed, and she wondered if he had slept all night with his neck at that awkward angle. *That boy will do anything to miss a day of school*, she thought.

A minute later, she heard a knock on the open door. Deacon Michael. When they made eye contact, a smile spread across his face, and Constance motioned for him to come on in.

"How you feelin' this mornin', Sister Constance?" he quietly spoke as he set down a vase of flowers on a nearby stand.

"I've been better, Michael. I've been better."

"You gave that boy there, quite a scare," he nodded toward Sonny still sleeping.

"Gave myself quite a scare, and I really don't remember what happened. I just blanked out."

"Had a mild stroke—that's what. But I imagine you'll be back to yourself in no time."

Would she be back to herself? She wondered. She knew too many people who had lost their independence after a stroke, and she didn't have time to be sitting around in no old folks home. Sonny needed her too much, and she was not going down without a fight.

As she tried to sit up, Deacon Michael rushed over to her side and pushed the button that raised the back of her bed. She noticed that she still had all her faculties and was thankful that she didn't sound like she was slurring her words.

"Can I get you anything?" Deacon Michael asked.

"Crushed ice would be nice."

In response, he patted Constance on the fingers, avoiding the IV taped to her hand and turned toward the door. He was a good friend—always willing and ready to help out when needed, and she couldn't help but think that her life would have been completely different had she married him.

* * *

Constance woke up a few hours later. The cup of ice that Deacon Michael had returned with had already melted. And he and Sonny were now passing the time, watching a court show blaring on the television. She cleared her throat to let them know she was awake, and both were at her bedside in an instant.

"Granny, you're awake?" Sonny nestled his face into her neck and kissed her cheek. It had been two days since she'd arrived to the hospital in the back of an ambulance.

"Yes, dear. I'm okay," she wrapped her free hand around his neck and pulled him close to look into his eyes. "Were you worried about me?"

He nodded as his eyes began to fill.

"Good. Maybe now you'll act right and do what I tell you to do," she patted him on the cheek, and he smiled.

"Constance, there's a bit of a crowd gathering in the corridor and waiting room. Is there anything you'd like me to tell them?" Deacon Michael asked.

"A crowd? What do you mean?"

"People from the church, a few of your old students, and a couple of your neighbors have come by to check on you. But you can't have that many people back here in the room. So, what do you want me to tell them?"

Constance wasn't feeling that well and was in no mood to entertain. Not to mention that she was worried that her hair was a mess and she didn't have the energy to fix herself up. "Please thank them for coming and for all the well wishes." Constance hesitated, "but I'm still feeling tired and I think I need to rest."

* * *

Deacon Michael headed toward the waiting room to carry out his marching orders, but ran into Pastor Andrews. To tell the truth, the man made his skin crawl. How he ignored his one grandson but preached forgiveness and love was beyond anything Deacon Michael could comprehend.

"Morning, Pastor," Deacon Michael nodded and moved to the left to make room for the other man to pass through.

"Hey, Michael. How are you?" Pastor Andrews reached over to give Deacon Michael a half-handshake/half-hug and patted him on the shoulder.

"Doing well. Just trying to make sure Constance and Sonny have everything they need," Deacon Michael cocked his head to the side and waited to see if Sonny's name would register with the pastor. It didn't. Or at least he didn't let on that it did.

"Heard half the congregation was here in the waiting room. So I figured I'd better come and see her too," Pastor Andrew nodded and smiled. (If there was one thing for which Pastor Andrews could be counted on, it was making and keeping up appearances.)

"Oh, of course, I was just getting ready to make an announcement about Constance. If you'd like to join me in the waiting room?" He held out his hand and motioned for Pastor Andrews to lead the way.

Pastor Andrews hesitated and then decided to move forward at Michael's invitation. As both men stepped into the waiting room, Deacon Michael motioned for the 40 or so people to gather around to hear an update on Constance's condition.

"Sister Constance is awake and..."

"Look at God!" someone shouted, and a few knowing "Amens" rippled through the crowd.

Deacon Michael smiled and continued in a loud whisper, "Constance is awake, but she is really weak. She asked me to thank y'all for coming to check on her and for making her hospital room look like a funeral home with all the flowers you sent."

A chuckle spread through the group.

"Truth be told, though, I don't think it's a good idea for her to have visitors. She's on the mend, but still very weak. So I'd like y'all to do me a favor and skip seeing her today."

"That's fine, Deacon. We just want what's best for Sister Constance," someone said.

"Yeah, that's fine. But let's close with a word of prayer. The Good Book says where two or three are gathered...so it wouldn't hurt for us to lift up Sister Jackson with a word before we head out," another in the group offered.

Deacon Michael raised his hand in a quieting motion and nodded in agreement. A word of prayer was always a good idea. "Let's bow our heads and pray. Our Father..."

"Actually, Deacon, I'd like to say the prayer before we head out." Pastor Andrews stepped forward and tapped him on the shoulder.

"Of course," Deacon Grimes clenched his jaw and bowed his head again to pray.

"Most Gracious Heavenly Father, King of the Universe and Almighty God, we come before you..."

Ten minutes later, Pastor Andrews ended with an "Amen" and an "Amen" and an "Amen."

"Thank you, Pastor, for that moving prayer," Deacon Grimes rubbed his temple and looked at his watch. "I'm sure there are a million things for you to do at the church. So...you have a blessed day, and I'll be in touch soon," he gave Pastor Andrews a strong pat on the shoulder and watched as the preacher moved toward the elevator begrudgingly.

Most of the Buchanan members continued to mill about in the waiting room, and Deacon Michael took the time to acknowledge the lingerers, promising he would pass along messages to Constance.

Minutes later, the waiting room was finally clear of Constance's well-wishers, and he was able to head back to her room.

* * *

"You'll never guess who showed up to make an appearance," Deacon Michael started his sentence before he was fully inside Constance's room.

"Who?"

"Pastor Andrews, knowing good and well he just showed up to be..."

"Dear, would you go and get me another cup of crushed ice?" Constance interrupted and handed her grandson the large, blue, plastic cup. "This one is completely melted," she smiled to say thank you.

Then she waited until Sonny was through the door and out of earshot. "Good grief, Michael, you know I don't like anyone to talk about Pastor Andrews around Sonny," her eyes narrowed. "The man has never taken an interest in him, and I never want Sonny to know who he really is. I couldn't take it if he knew that Pastor Andrews wanted nothing to do with him."

"Well, why do you stay at Buchanan then, Connie?"

No one had called her that in a long time. She'd thought about that question a thousand times—why not just start over and leave Buchanan? But she could never leave. The congregation, long before Pastor Andrews had shown up, had been everything to her.

"Because it is the only real family I've ever had," her eyes filled with water as she remembered sitting in the church office with Pastor Strong and his wife, Sister Shirley.

She was a sophomore at Fisk University when her world had come crashing down. Carrying Victor Senior's child, she decided to call her parents, and that's when they told her she was on her own. The Strongs then paid for her school the next semester and organized a small wedding for her and Victor. No—she wasn't going anywhere. Buchanan was her home, and she would never leave it, no matter whose name was on the marquee.

Deacon Michael nodded knowingly and settled back into the recliner in the corner of the room. He understood that Constance was remembering and retracing the path that had led her to Buchanan, and he wanted to give her time to reflect.

"What do you think about us taking a trip out West?" Constance changed the subject.

"Out West?" Michael sat up in his chair.

"Yeah, to the old homestead."

"Hmm. For what?"

"To visit. Take Sonny. See what has changed."

Constance had never once mentioned going back to Wharton in the almost 50 years she had lived in Nashville. Michael had been back occasionally. But once his parents had passed, there was really no other reason to go back. He wondered why Constance was so keen on visiting the place. For all she knew, there might be nothing left of the homestead.

"Okay," he shrugged. "If that's what you want."

"It's what I *need* to do, Michael," she let her gaze fall on him. "It's what I *need* to do. It's time for me to let go of some things. And I don't know any other way to do it. Besides, Sonny needs to know where his people are from."

He understood. Constance needed to forgive.

"Okay. Sure. I'll drive y'all out there. Maybe that'll give you some incentive to rest up and get yourself out of here."

"Got your ice, Granny," Sonny said as he appeared in the doorway.

"Thank you, dear. Just put it there on the stand." She motioned toward the piece of furniture. "What do you think about us taking a trip once I get out of here?"

"A trip?" Sonny's head jerked back.

"Yes, a trip. What is it with y'all?" Constance looked back at Michael. "I'd like to take you to Texas and show you where I grew up. It'll be good for you to know a little about your history."

Sonny shrugged.

"If you behave, I'll throw in a trip to Six Flags on the way back. But *only* if you behave and promise not to worry me all the way there."

Sonny's eyes widened, then he pumped his fist in the air. "Yes! When we goin'?"

Constance and Deacon Michael burst out laughing.

"How about during spring break? I should be all better by then, and you'll be out of school for a week."

Sonny leaned in to give her a kiss on the cheek. "Okay then, Granny. I'm gonna help take good care of you. The faster you get better, the quicker I can get to Six Flags." He pulled the hospital blanket up around Constance's lap and settled into his recliner in the corner of the room.

* * *

Back home, Sonny sat on the edge of her bed and read the last verse of Proverbs 25 to Constance. "He that hath no rule over his own spirit is like a city that is broken down, and without walls." Then he closed the big family Bible he'd taken from the coffee table in the living room and muttered, "Bless the reading of God's Word."

"You finished your homework?"

"Yes, Granny."

"Okay, I'm just checking. Taking care of me is no excuse for your grades to be falling. Getting a good education is your only…"

"…chance to be something is this world," Sonny finished her sentence and stood up to look her in the face. "Granny, you've said that at least a million times. Will you just relax and let me take care of you? For once I know what I'm doing."

Constance dismissed that logic with a wave of her hand and settled into the pillows Sonny had positioned behind her. "All right. But I'm still in charge. As long as I have breath in my body, there is only one boss in the Jackson household."

Sonny chuckled to himself. Sick as she was, Constance still wasn't giving up control of anything. "Yes, Granny. You are still the boss," he kissed her on the forehead and tucked the comforter around her chin. "I'll fix you breakfast tomorrow morning before I go to school, okay?"

"Thank you, son. Don't forget to say your prayers before you go to sleep."

"Yeees, Granny. Good night." He flipped the light off as he walked out of the room and pulled the door almost shut. He went to the kitchen to wash and put away the dinner dishes. Constance had eaten hardly anything, and Sonny wondered if he should tell the doctor who had told him to monitor her appetite.

Twenty minutes later, Sonny gave the room one last look-over to make sure it was cleaned to his Granny's satisfaction. The counters had been wiped, the floor swept, the sink completely clear, and the dishes put away.

Before climbing into bed, he knelt beside it and mumbled, "Please take care of Granny. I need her." No other words came to his mind, so he climbed into bed and tried to shut out the day.

I'm with you, Sonny thought he heard.

No one's really listening.

Then he drifted off to sleep.

* * *

As days slipped into weeks, Constance spent more and more time in bed. She'd even missed church two weeks in a row. Sonny wondered if anyone was listening up there or if it even mattered. Deacon Michael came by to bring communion and to pray. But Constance didn't get better. Sonny got into the habit of checking on Constance in the middle of the night, and when he went to bed each night, he turned to set his alarm clock for 1:00 a.m.

CHAPTER NINETEEN

Sonny's lips pressed together in a tight white line, and his steps quickened as he crossed the street. There she was, in a dress that was too short for a mother and wearing clear, platform high heels. Rachel was leaning inside the passenger's side of a green Thunderbird, talking to a middle-aged balding man.

Sonny hadn't seen his mother in two years—since his eleventh birthday party to be exact—but he'd recognize her anywhere. Her green eyes with that blank stare, the dark roots of her now blond hair, and her ever-growing collection of tattoos that colored her white skin olive.

There she was—the woman who had left him and had never looked back. At times, he would think about what he would do if he ever saw her. Now, he had his chance.

Sonny slammed his fist on the hood of the Thunderbird. Then he stood perfectly still and glared at Rachel and the male driver.

Both the man and Rachel jerked their attention to the hood of the car, while the man's grip tightened on the wheel and Rachel stood up cautiously, pulling down on her dress, then scratching at her elbow. Sonny had her undivided attention, for once, and he would not let the moment pass.

She met his gaze slowly and noticed that the way he was standing there reminded her of Victor Junior. Her head tilted slightly as she tried to hear what Vic would have said to her in this moment. He had always known what to do or say, even in the stickiest of situations.

He would have probably said something like, 'It'll all work, just be cool.' He had always thought that everything would end up okay. But nothing had. Their son was standing here as living proof of that. Sonny looked down at her. Although only 13, he towered a full three inches taller. He grabbed Rachel's wrist and then flung her away from the car.

"Sonny! Sonny, what are you doing here?" Rachel said as she reached out and tried to touch his face. He jerked his head back and gave her a sour look.

"Woman, I don't know where your hands have been. Don't you ever try to touch me again!" He took a step back from her. So many nights, he had wondered why she had never come to pick him up, never called him, and probably never even thought about him. Now, he knew the answer. She was a mess.

She'd lost a lot of weight and there were marks on her arms. Her eyes had that dull look—but he still recognized them. Her eyes were his eyes—and one of the reasons girls were so drawn to him. The man in the Thunderbird started up his car and drove away.

Sonny clenched his fist, and the vein in his forehead began to pop. His mother couldn't even look him in the eye now. She just focused on the cracks in the pavement. She didn't see him. She didn't care. And he understood that that was the way things would always be.

"My life is all your fault. You hear me? It's all your fault. You left me."

"Yeah. Yeah, I know," Rachel mumbled as she traced the cracks on the sidewalk with her heel. "I just can't seem to..."

"Don't talk to me," Sonny screamed. "Don't you say another word!" He shoved Rachel, and she fell to the ground.

Her shoulders began to shake as she let out a sob, "I'm sorry! Okay, I'm sorry. I'm no good. I was no good for your father and no good for you. You're better off without me. Can't you see that?" Rachel wrapped her arms around her shoulders.

"Yeah, I can see that," Sonny spit in Rachel's direction. "And I never want to see you again. Just do what you do best—and leave."

* * *

Sonny left Rachel in a puddle on the pavement and headed home. He thought about all the moments that she'd missed. She hadn't been there when Constance collapsed on the floor—when the only person who cared anything about him was almost ripped away.

She hadn't been there the day he scored for the other team and every person in the gym, including Constance, had erupted in laughter. She didn't know that he and Carlos had cut school for two weeks. She didn't even know Carlos.

Sonny turned around slowly and walked back home to Constance.

All this time, he'd been wondering where Rachel was. Turns out, she wasn't far. But at the same time, she wasn't close either.

Sonny noticed a blackbird sitting alone on a power line, and felt just like it—and more alone than ever.

She said she was sorry. But she didn't even know what she was sorry for. Didn't matter. He would never forgive her. She didn't deserve to live. Maybe one day, she would just stop breathing. Or worse. It would serve her right. He was better off without her, and Rachel wasn't worth worrying about anyway.

Sonny jerked a branch from an overgrown tree and noticed that the street lights were beginning to flicker. They would be shining bright in a few minutes. And that meant that he had to get home or Constance would be waiting on the porch with her arms crossed asking why he was late. At least she worried about him and wondered where he was at night. That was more than he could say for Rachel.

He pushed over a neighbor's trash can on the way home, then smiled to himself as he watched it topple over and the mess spread across the sidewalk. Someone would have to clean it up. But it wouldn't be him.

You've got Carlos.

He *did* have Carlos. There was something about being with him that made him feel a little bit taller, a little bit stronger, and a little less afraid. Carlos wouldn't let anything happen to him, and if anything did happen, at least he wouldn't be alone.

* * *

Sonny brushed by Constance and barely said a word when he got home. He sat down at the piano and played for an hour and then asked to be excused from dinner.

That worried Constance, because it was unlike him to ever pass up a meal. Come what may, he was always hungry. But tonight, he had come home and made music rather than the usual habit of consuming it through his earphones. He said he wasn't feeling well, which Constance found hard to believe.

After Sonny went to his room, Constance wore a path in the living room carpet, trying to figure out what was the matter with that boy. And when she couldn't hear footsteps in his room any longer, she crept up the stairs and quietly moved her rocking chair into his room. He was sound asleep and snoring like a hog in heat, but it didn't bother her. When Victor Senior had been alive, he had snored the same way, but Constance never seemed to miss a minute of sleep.

She positioned her rocking chair as close to Sonny's bed as she could and leaned toward him to whisper a prayer over his resting soul. The dazed look she saw in his eyes when he had come home bothered her. She'd seen that look on his father's face 15 years ago. But she'd been too preoccupied to seek out the source of his worries.

That wouldn't happen again.

Constance stretched her hands out and hovered over Sonny's back as she addressed the enemy of his soul head on, "You took my son. But you will not take my grandson. You hear me? You will not take him."

Even as Constance challenged the attacker, her memories flashed back to the time Victor Junior occupied this room. Jordan posters had covered every wall. And no matter how often she had changed his sheets and scoured the room for his uniforms, his room always smelled like a gym. At least Sonny was tidier than Victor Junior.

She tried to refocus her mind and began to pray. This battle was real, and she knew it wasn't going to be easy. Constance sighed, "Lord, You gotta help me with this boy. He wants to be good. Help him. Help me, help him. If you never do nothing else for me, You owe me this one. I go to church regularly and even Baptist Training sometimes. I usher, and I pray." Constance sank back into her rocking chair. "I've been faithful, now the rest is up to You. You owe me."

A chill invaded Sonny's room even though all the windows were closed, and Constance woke up from her praying nap. The Bone

Thugs-N-Harmony poster fluttered on the wall, and Sonny's backpack fell to the floor. Out dropped a small sandwich bag of marijuana. Constance hugged herself with both arms and then rubbed her eyes.

She knew the shadow of the curse was lurking but didn't expect it to be so soon. Not this close. He was still so young. Constance had done everything that she knew to do. Still, she wanted more time. But the enemy was already coming.

* * *

As she closed the door, Constance noticed the dust on the baseboard outside Sonny's room and made a mental note to do some cleaning the next day. Then she paused in the hallway, thinking about the times she used to creep up those same steps to pray over Victor Junior after he'd gone to sleep. It hadn't saved him. Maybe it wouldn't work for Sonny either.

Something was changing with him, but Constance couldn't put her finger on it. Lately, she found herself asking him to do things more than once. And sometimes he even had the nerve to glare at her. Victor Junior never would have tried her like that. But she was younger and stronger then.

She eased her way down the steps and stopped to look at her collection of family portraits. None of those pictures told the real story. Olan Mills had a way of capturing every family picture-perfect and leaving all the brokenness outside the frame.

Tonight, she peered into a family portrait where Victor Junior sat between her and Victor Senior. That space on the wall had been empty for years. Victor Junior's little legs were crossed Indian style, and he wore the powder-blue suit and bow tie she'd gotten him that year for Easter.

Victor Senior had joined them at church that Easter Sunday. He was a "CME" attender, darkening the doors of Buchanan only on Christmas, Mother's Day, and Easter. But the members always treated him as if he was the head trustee. Constance would smile and nod when they welcomed him as a regular member.

That picture was almost 30 years old, looking back, she decided that she would have done a lot of things differently. But she'd done the best she could with the cards that she'd been dealt. She straightened the picture on the wall and took a deep breath. She'd continue to pray and do her best with Sonny. That's all she could do. It was all she had left to give.

Constance changed into her satin nightgown and decided to skip her nighttime skin-care routine. She just didn't have it in her to cleanse, tone, and moisturize. She didn't even have the energy to kneel for her prayers tonight.

She slipped on her satin bonnet, climbed into bed, and pulled the floral comforter up over her face. Her limbs felt heavy, and she lay there quietly as she tried to figure out what to say to God.

Minutes passed as she retraced the happy times she'd had as a mother and the good times she'd experienced as a grandmother. She also remembered the feeling of being on the edge of madness when all of it had been ripped away. She simply could not bear to face that again.

Constance choked back the feelings that were gathering in her throat, "Father, help me get it right this time."

CHAPTER TWENTY

D eacon Michael came prepared to entertain two kids for the road trip out West, and he was bound and determined to teach Sonny and Paige the meaning of "real music." Constance had invited Paige, Sonny's half-sister, to join them. She felt he needed someone near his age to talk to, and who better than his own sister.

The fact was, they hadn't seen each other in years. And Constance wasn't quite sure whether or not either of them remembered the time their mother had taken them on vacation to Panama City. It had been a long time ago. But she still remembered Sonny's face when Rachel dropped him off and left with Paige in tow. He had cried for hours and banged on the screen door, willing her to come back. She hadn't.

He was six back then, and Constance wouldn't let Rachel visit for a long time after that. It was just too hard on him. He melted into a puddle whenever she left, and Constance hated being the one left to pick up the pieces and explain why he couldn't go and live with his mother. Truth was, Rachel wasn't fit to be a mother. Constance always said, "Just because you can make a baby, doesn't make you qualified to raise one."

A few months after their trip to Panama City, someone told Constance that Paige had been taken into state custody. The story was, a neighbor found her at home alone one night. Rachel had snuck out after Paige had fallen asleep, and when she came back home the next morning, the authorities were waiting for her. Of course, Rachel was high and drunk. God only knew what she'd spent the night doing. Thankfully, Paige landed in a foster home with a good Christian couple, and they eventually adopted her.

Marvin Gaye's voice filled the car, interrupting Constance's thoughts.

"Listen baby. Ain't no mountain high. Ain't no valley low. Ain't no river wide enough...." She turned the volume up and leaned over into the back seat, singing the words to Paige and Sonny. "If you need me, call me, no matter where you are, no matter how far...."

Sonny and Paige looked at each other and instantly busted into a fit of laughter as they watched Constance bop along to the music. Deacon Michael joined in the singing while also attempting to dance in the driver's seat, and the kids kept right on laughing. Once the song ended, they gave a courtesy round of applause.

"Y'all want to play a game?"

"Depends. What kind of game?" Sonny asked.

"Depends on what?" Deacon Michael looked in the rearview mirror to make eye contact with Sonny.

"Whether or not your game is boring."

"Hmm. Well, the winner of this game gets a twenty-dollar prize... whether the game is boring or not."

"I'm playing, Deacon Michael. Forget Sonny." Paige leaned into the front seat and tapped him on the shoulder.

"All right then, Paige. It's called..."

"Wait. I'm playing too," Sonny interrupted.

"Thought you'd change your tune." A smiled slipped across Deacon Michael's lips. "Nothing like a little motivation...is there, Constance?"

Constance shook her head and looked out the window at the flat brown plains with speckles of green as far as she could see. The land was so dry and empty. Every now and then, she would see a pump jack on the horizon. Other than that, nothing much had changed along this stretch of highway since she had left for Nashville on a Greyhound bus all those years ago.

The pump jacks reminded her of the days she and her mother would take lunch to her father down at the oil rig. They didn't go often, but whenever the opportunity arose, she always liked seeing her dad at work. A quiet man, but at the oil rig, he was the boss.

As a girl, she loved watching how the men responded to him, saying, "Yes, Sir." Far different than how he acted when they went into town once a month, and the store owner's daughter had the nerve to address him by his first name. She hated that he answered her with a "Yes, ma'am," while never looking her in the eye.

Years later, when she called to tell her parents that she was pregnant during her second Fall at Fisk, her father hadn't said anything. She couldn't remember what her mother had said. She just knew that she was on her own from that point on. They'd let go of her—when she needed them the most.

You must forgive, the voice reminded her.

She knew that. She knew she needed to let go of everything. It would be good to go to the old homestead. To remember the good times and let go of all the pain she'd been holding on to. She was grateful Victor Senior had been gone a long time. But the wounds were still fresh from Victor Junior's death. The 10 years that had passed hadn't helped to erase the pain. Her heart ripped the day he was murdered, and she wasn't sure she'd ever recover.

Sonny's voice interrupted her thoughts.

" 'Q' on that truck's license plate," Sonny pointed to the eighteen-wheeler coming toward them on the other side of the road.

"There ain't no 'Q' on that license plate," Paige frowned as the truck drew closer.

"Just wanted to call it out in case there was."

Paige rolled her eyes and hit Sonny on the shoulder. "You need to quit trying to cheat all the time."

He looked at her and smiled. Then he leaned into the front seat and whispered to Constance, "Love you, Granny, and thanks for bringing Paige."

Constance pressed her cheek against his and said, "No problem, son. I'm glad you're having fun." She took a deep breath and relaxed her head against the head rest. Something about this moment and this trip...it just felt right.

* * *

Deacon Michael pulled up to the Phillips 66 and pressed the button to open his fuel flap. "Okay, troops. Let's take a 20-minute leg-and-bathroom break. Be back in the car at 14:00 hours."

"What time is that?" Paige said.

"Two o'clock," Sonny answered without thinking.

"Oh. Okay."

Deacon Michael pumped the gas as Sonny and Paige went into the convenience store to use the restroom and restock on candy. Constance spent the time inside the empty car, clearing out the trash and straightening the pillows and blankets they'd brought along with them. She waited until everyone returned to the car, then headed into the convenience store for her turn using the facilities.

"Wait. I'll go with you, Granny."

"Boy, I am fine to go into the store by myself."

"It's not you I'm worried about," he held the door open for Constance as she walked into the store. "I'll wait for you here," he nodded at the group of burly-looking men in the corner and crossed his arms over his chest.

"All right then, son." Constance smiled to herself as she turned to head toward the restroom and thought, *What is he going to do if those guys in the corner do try some foolishness?*

A few minutes later, Constance came out to find Sonny still standing guard. She picked up a few snacks, paid for them, and stuffed the goodies in her brown shoulder bag.

"Would you like to take a little walk with me? I need to stretch my legs a bit more," she said.

"Okay." Sonny opened the door and motioned for Constance to lead the way.

After looking left and then right, Constance decided to walk toward the stop light of this small town which stood roadside to Highway 59. There were only a handful of buildings, and most of them looked to be deserted. But it was nice to fill her lungs with a bit more fresh air before cramming back into the car to finish the last stretch of the trip.

"Granny, why are we taking this trip?"

"What do you mean, 'why are we taking this trip'? To get away. Relax. So you can learn more about your family history."

"See, that's what I'm talking about. You've never really talked about where you grew up."

"Yes. I know. I'm trying to change that."

"So why now?"

"When I was in the hospital, I realized I've been holding on to some things for a long time. Some anger for things my parents did."

"What did your parents do? You never talk about them."

"It's not so much what they did. It's more what they didn't do. When I needed them the most, they turned their backs on me, and basically said I was on my own," Constance bit down on her bottom lip and for an instant and relived the years of fending for herself. She wiped her cheek with the back of her hand and looked down the street of what was probably once a vibrant little town.

"Let's find somewhere to sit," she reached for Sonny's elbow and motioned toward one of the store windowsills that seemed just wide enough to be used as a bench.

Sonny nodded and moved toward the spot. They settled in, Constance took a deep breath and began.

"Homecoming of 1958—I met your granddad at the dance. He was the finest man there, and I was all in a tizzy when he asked to dance with me. Of course, I played it cool."

Sonny winced at his grandmother's attempt at using slang.

"It's true. I couldn't let him think that I fancied him. That would have been un-ladylike, and he was supposed to chase me a little."

Sonny rolled his eyes and tried to pin himself to his seat. It felt odd for his grandmother to be talking to him like this.

"The thing is…two months later…I wound up pregnant. I didn't say 'no' long enough." She let her eyes connect with Sonny and hoped he was picking up what she was putting down. "The whole life I'd been dreaming of and working toward was reshuffled based on one stupid decision. I called my parents asking what I should do, and they basically said I was on my own."

"What did you do?"

"I went to the church to talk to the pastor and his wife, and they told me to marry Victor. They promised to pay for my Spring semester, and they hosted a small wedding for us. Two months later, I had a miscarriage. At the time, it felt like I was being given another chance to pursue my dreams. But I was still tied to your grandfather, and I wouldn't go back on the vow I made to God. So, I was angry. Angry at my parents for not helping me. Angry at Victor for not being who I thought he should be. Angry at myself for throwing everything away."

Sonny didn't appear to be listening anymore. Constance recognized the dazed look in his eyes, and she knew it was probably too much for him to digest. But, she continued.

"I almost did the same thing to your father that my parents did to me…when he told me you were coming." That got his attention. Sonny leaned toward Constance, and he appeared to be hungry for whatever came next.

"Yes, I almost did the same thing. Turned away from my only son when he needed me the most. I was so upset with him. Just like me, he gave up his chance to do something that mattered. But I couldn't let him live with the same pain of rejection that I'd endured. I'm just not made of that material," she patted him on the knee and forced a smile. "But look at us now, on the road again to where it all began."

Sonny rested his head between the crook of Constance's neck and shoulder. "What was my dad like?" his voice cracked before he could finish the question.

Constance hesitated and thought hard before she answered.

"Your father was strong, in mind and in body. When he made up his mind to do something that was it. One summer, he cut every yard in the neighborhood just so he could have enough money to buy your mother a nice birthday present. He could have been anything," Constance rested her head on his.

"You're a lot like him, you know. Kind and loyal, sometimes to a fault." She sat up straight and looked him in the eye. "But you also got something you need to get rid of, Sonny. I know you know what I'm talking about."

He let out a long slow breath and answered, "I know. I know, Granny."

"It's one thing to know. But it's another thing to do. That's the problem I have with you. I don't see you doing. You are so sweet and helpful one day; then a couple days around that boy, Carlos, and you are a completely different person. You know I'm telling the truth."

Sonny didn't respond.

Constance sensed him shutting down and said a silent prayer—that some of what she was saying would stay with him. She just didn't know how much time she had to keep repeating herself. One day, he would be on his own, and if he didn't straighten up, he would end up just like his father. A good boy who fell victim to his decisions.

"Come on. Let's head back toward the car. Deacon Michael and Paige are probably wondering where we are."

Sonny nodded and helped Constance to her feet. Once she was stable, he reached down and wrapped his arms around her.

"Love you, Granny."

"I love you too," she pushed him back so she could look into his face. "I hope you know, I just want what's best for you. I just want you to be okay."

"Yeah. I know," he wrapped his arm around her shoulder, and they walked back to the car.

CHAPTER TWENTY-ONE

Constance felt as if she were traveling back in time as they neared her childhood home. Although almost 50 years had passed, nothing much seemed to have changed on U.S. Highway 59—other than the Standard Oil sign on the neighbor's barn appeared a bit more faded, and the barn itself, once a cherry red, was now a graying wood color. On closer inspection, however, Constance thought that one good strong wind might blow the building over.

Deacon Michael slowed his red Cadillac Seville to a snail's pace, turned onto the dirt road, and drove even more carefully down the lane to the homestead. His once shiny car was no longer shiny after having traveled the 836 miles from Nashville to their destination in Wharton, Texas.

As the 30-by-30 white clapboard house trimmed in a dull burgundy came into view, Constance was flooded with a sense of warmth and connection that she hadn't felt in a very long time. The only thing missing was the sounds. The screams of her younger brother and sisters pushing each other on the tire swing in the woods behind the house. The constant clickety-clack of freight cars moving down the railroad across the lane. The conversation and laughter of her family sitting on the porch while the girls braided each other's hair and everyone watched those trains go by.

Deacon Michael parked the car, and Constance opened her door even before she unbuckled her seat belt. Home. After all these years. She hadn't been here since the age of 16 when she went away to college. The plan had been to earn a teaching degree and then come back to teach at the all-black high school. But those plans had changed when she met Victor Senior, and her life became something she never thought it would be.

During the first few years away, every so often, she would receive a letter from her mother with an update on her siblings. But the letters never mentioned her father, and she knew that he was still angry.

But that didn't matter now. She was home, and in this moment, it felt different. Decades of distance seemed to have washed away the pain, replaced now with all the memories—smells of chow-chow and hog-head cheese coming from the kitchen, sounds of Sam Cooke ringing through the house, constant visits from friends and strangers alike—even the hobos from off a train car were welcomed by her mother.

When Constance was a young girl, all she could think about was getting out of Wharton. But now that she was much older and the years ahead of her were far less than the years behind her, she thought mostly of the happy times. Her life had been filled with good things, like Friday-night fish fries, picking pecans, and watching black-and-white westerns on her grandparents' television set.

The shouts of Sonny and Paige snatched Constance from her reflections and back to the present moment. She looked across the grassless yard to see the two running around like wild banshees, and she couldn't help smiling as she watched Sonny chase his half-sister.

Paige's adopted family had reached out the year before, expressing their desire for Paige to have a relationship with her brother. As a result, the Jacksons and the Sneeds met once a month for lunch after church so that Sonny and Paige could spend some time together.

Constance took in a deep breath as she climbed the steps to the front porch. The porch swing was still there, but instead of hanging from the rafters, it was laying on the rotted floor. The chains had rusted and broken years ago.

How many summer nights did I sit on that swing with my mother? And how often did I wish to be back here when things got tough with Victor Senior?

"Sonny! Paige! Come here, please." Constance called as she settled into the sole chair that still occupied the porch.

"Yes, Granny?" Sonny said. Face flushed, he rested his hands on his knees and tried to catch his breath after chasing Paige.

"Sonny, in the woods behind the house, there used to be a tire swing. Take Paige back there, and you two, go and play. I want to sit in the quiet for a while. Y'all are kicking up enough noise to raise the dead."

"Okay, Granny," Sonny said as his shoulders slumped. He and Paige had been pretty good for the 13-hour car ride, and they only wanted to play outside.

He turned around and shoved Paige in the shoulder. "Granny said for us to go and play on the tire swing while she looks around the house."

"Oh, okay. But if you know what's good for you...you betta not push me again."

Raising his eyebrows, Sonny looked at Paige as if to say, "Really?"

In turn, Paige glared back at him and balled up her fist. For a short, chubby girl, Paige had grit, and Sonny liked her for that.

"Okay, I'll push you on the tire swing. Come on." He pulled Paige's plait and sped off toward the woods.

Whap! A few seconds later, she landed a smack across his back, just as she had promised. And Sonny had to laugh.

During the next few minutes, both of them searched through all kinds of old vines and trash that had been dumped in the woods, and then finally, found the tire swing. The tire must have been taken from a tractor, judging from its size, and it looked like it had been hanging on that old tree for a long time. The rope, on the other hand, was still the thickness of Sonny's wrist. He tilted his head, it seemed safe enough.

"Jump in. I'll push you," Sonny said as he held the swing to the side so she could climb in. Paige's face lit up, and she put her foot on Sonny's knee and used his shoulder to steady herself.

The sensation of flying hit her as Sonny pushed her faster and higher. Having a brother felt good. For a while, Paige had been bounced around foster homes, but now, she had a mom and dad who loved her and an older brother who was fun.

Paige could feel her stomach flip every time she swung up and then back again. It was a good feeling, mixed with the thought that she could almost touch the branches.

"Higher, Sonny! Higher!"

Sonny let out a grunt. Pushing Paige's heavy self plus the tire, wore him out. Sweat collected around his collar and began to show through his shirt. But pushing her was fun, especially when he pushed harder and Paige yelled when the tire jumped when reaching the top.

"Okay, a couple more minutes. Then that's it. I'm tired."

"Okay. Okay. Just a few more minutes," Paige begged.

Sonny wondered if he could push Paige so hard she'd swing around the entire branch in a full circle. She had good speed, and she was already going higher than the branch that the swing was tied to.

He decided to go for it.

"I'm gonna make you go all the way around!" he yelled excitedly.

"What!? No! I don't think that's a..."

Crack! The next thing Sonny saw was the branch splitting and then crashing toward him. He managed to dive out of the way and closed his eyes just as Paige banged into the trunk of the old oak.

When he opened his eyes, Paige lay there in a pile on the ground. He rushed over to her and held his breath. *What if she's dead?* he thought, as he remembered how hard her head had hit the tree.

"Paige, can you hear me?" Sonny said in a cautious whisper while patting her face. Paige didn't move, and her leg was bent awkwardly beneath her.

"Paige, please don't be dead. Granny will kill me." Sonny sent up a quick prayer and crossed himself, like he'd seen Sonny Corleone, do in *The Godfather*. Suddenly, Paige let out a giggle, and a smile spread across her face as her eyes popped open.

"Get off-a-me, Sonny! I could-a died, and all you can think about is what Grandma Constance would do to you?" Paige got up slowly and dusted the dirt off of her light purple culottes.

Sonny sat there and stared blankly at her—for what seemed like several minutes. He couldn't find the words to express his relief. At the same time, he couldn't understand what had happened. He'd heard her hit the tree going full-speed, and then, she'd hit the ground like a ton of bricks. How come she was acting like nothing happened?

"Are you okay?" Sonny eventually choked out, while they both stood and he began to pat her on the shoulder and pull leaves and dirt out of her hair.

"Leave me alone," Paige said as she brushed his hands away from her. "I'm fine. Will you quit being so dramatic? I didn't even hit the tree."

"I saw you hit the tree! Wha-d'ya mean you 'didn't hit the tree'?"

"I did not hit the tree. I just fell. Quit being a sissy, and let's go tell Grandma Constance we're hungry." Paige turned and headed toward the house, leaving Sonny standing there, still trying to process what had just happened.

Something was weird about Paige—he just couldn't quite put his finger on it.

* * *

It's good to be home, thought Constance. She had already taken a tour of the house and was now walking down the hallway where her many high school awards had once decorated the walls—the state degree, the honor ribbons, and the home economics certificates. When she came to the very back of the house, she stood still and looked into an empty and tattered area that had once been her old bedroom. A room that had provided protection and shelter for four chatty little girls with big dreams for the future.

Now, all those things were gone. But the memories stayed, that and the field mice.

CHAPTER TWENTY-TWO

The trip back to Nashville seemed to take half the time it took to get to Wharton. Before they knew it, Deacon Michael pulled up to the curb in front of Constance's home, and everyone tumbled out of the car. The journey to Texas and back had been good, but being out of the car was better. Paige's parents were sitting on the porch, reading books and waiting for their arrival.

After Sonny helped Paige get her bag out of the trunk, he walked up the sidewalk with her toward her parents and watched as her dad jumped off the porch to pick her up and swing her around. Her mom stroked her hair and kissed her on the forehead.

So that's what it's like to have parents, huh? Sonny shifted from one foot to the other and tried not to stare.

"Daddy, will you put me down for a second?" Paige said. Her dad lowered her to the ground, and Paige walked over to Sonny standing on the grass. He was strangely quiet for once, looking at his feet and shifting side to side. And no attempts were made to hit, poke, or pull her hair.

"You sad to see me go?" Paige said with her usual sass.

"Nah. Just waiting for you to take your bag," he said without looking up. He'd taken a shine to Paige over the past week and a half, and it had been nice to have someone around other than Constance.

"Oh, well, okay then," Paige took her bag from Sonny. "Imma miss you, okay? And I'm gonna pray for you every night. It was fun having a big brother for a while."

Paige reached in to wrap her arms around Sonny's neck and squeezed him. He patted her on the back and tried to get out of her grip. Hugs weren't really his thing.

"I love you, brother," Paige said.

He continued to pat Paige awkwardly on the back. He didn't know what to say. She, on the other hand, seemed so close and comfortable with him, even though they'd met only a few months ago.

Sonny unlocked the front door to the house and turned to wave from behind the screen door as Paige and her parents loaded up their car and escaped back to the suburbs.

CHAPTER TWENTY-THREE

Sonny tasted the blood pooling in his mouth as he readied for the next blow and tried to focus on who had just hit him. There were three of them, but his eyes couldn't make out their faces.

His leg muscles tightened as he resisted the instinct to run. If he did that, they would never stop coming. And he couldn't risk being punked. A beat-down was better.

So, he clenched his fists and started to windmill. Soon, the blows stopped raining down. His offense—answering the taunt of being a crack baby with the ultimate act of disrespect—a mother insult.

"Yo Mama." That's all Sonny had said.

A reflex. He hadn't even looked over his shoulder or broken his stride when he said it. Somebody had said he was a crack baby, and Sonny just responded.

Now, he couldn't take it back, and he was outnumbered. The fact that he had no crew and walked to school alone already made him an easy target. And...it didn't help that he was high yellow and had hair that waved without the help of Dax and a satin night cap.

Just stay up.

His heart pounded in his ears as he fought to stand. Something clicked in his chest at the feeling of his own blood being taken, and he would give them something extra to go along with their theft.

Anthony, one of the older boys from the block, came and mercifully tore them apart. "Hey, hey, hey! Y'all better quit for somebody call five-oh."

The boys' faces were flushed as they picked up backpacks and books that'd been scattered in the scuffle, anger seeped out the center of their eyes.

Anthony pushed one of the boys in the forehead and motioned for all three to take the long way to school. Sonny tightened the straps on his backpack and felt his cheek for proof of the fight. Someone had gotten a good lick in, but he'd made them pay.

"You held your own, little man," Anthony said as he reached down to dap Sonny, and Sonny smiled while straightening his pant leg.

He *had* held his own. Most importantly, he'd stayed up. They would be back, though, and there would be more of them next time.

But he wasn't gonna be an easy target. Not anymore.

* * *

The summer ended, and since Constance hadn't been feeling well, Sonny had picked up more than his usual chores around the house. Thankfully, he had inherited his work ethic from his dad, and Victor Junior had inherited it from his.

The bell on the front door of McPherson's Dry Cleaners clanged when Sonny yanked it open, and the smell of chemicals and standing hot air smacked him in the face.

He'd already spent four hours spring cleaning the house this morning, just the way he saw his granny do it—washing the baseboards, vacuuming the curtains, and cleaning behind the furniture. And Sonny hated it.

But house chores and cleaning were better than sitting still and watching his grandmother struggling to breathe and stay comfortable. At least he was doing something.

He slid the dry-cleaning ticket across the counter to the gray-haired woman sitting at the register. She watched an old-school TV with a rabbit-ears antenna, covered in foil that held it all together.

"Don't you know how to speak to your elders?" Sally said. She looked at him over her thick-rimmed glasses and frowned. "That's what's wrong with you young people today. Just come in here and hand me a ticket like you own the place."

Sally got up from her soap-watching perch and leaned on the counter to steady herself. She was gonna take her sweet time finding Constance's clothes.

"Miss. You need help findin' my granny's stuff?" Sonny said as he banged his knuckles on the counter and shifted his weight from one foot to the other. He was supposed to meet Carlos at Hartman at 3:45 to hoop. If they weren't first on the court, they'd have to wait to get picked. Didn't nobody have time for that.

"No, I do not. I been running this drycleaners for 30 years, and I do not need a knothead like you helping me do nothing," Sally poked her head between two sets of plastic-bagged shirts to fuss at him.

Sonny's eyes narrowed, and he kicked the bottom of the counter with his Lugz boot, leaving a long black mark.

"Look, just gimme my Granny's stuff so I can be out." He was sick and tired of old people talkin' down to him all the time. *Why do they always want respect, but give none?* he thought.

Sally found Constance's freshly dry-cleaned church clothes and hobbled back over to the counter. "That'll be $17.93," she held out her palm and opened the cash register with a clang.

Sonny looked at her hand, then grabbed the clothes on the hangers, and left—slamming the door on his way out.

He was keeping that $17.93 Constance had given him to pay for her dry cleaning. Served Sally right for talking crazy.

CHAPTER TWENTY-FOUR

C onstance had promised to take the boys to the local water park after school, because they had kept up their end of the bargain. That is, Sonny had gotten good grades, and Carlos hadn't failed any classes.

The bell rang at the end of the school day, and both boys knew they were just minutes from splashing around in the pool.

Sonny and Carlos stood in line ready to board the school bus, when someone tapped Carlos on the shoulder with the barrel of a pistol and pointed it directly at him. It was Robert. He had been an eighth-grader two years ago.

Sonny's leg muscles tightened, and in his mind he tried to run for cover. But his feet were stuck to the pavement as if he had been poured there with the concrete. Carlos slowly raised his hands toward heaven.

"You know I missed Halloween because of you, right?" Robert said.

"Maann, what is you even talkin' about?" Carlos's mind raced, searching for the right thing to say.

"You turned me in. Remember?" Robert held up his pants with his free hand and began circling Carlos. "Wait. Don't tell me you don't remember?"

Sonny stood two feet away and kept looking behind his shoulder. Someone had to see this. Someone had to come help. But everything was blurry. He turned back around and looked directly at Carlos's face and then at the pistol pointed at his chest.

"Hey," Carlos lowered his hands a little. "I did what I had to do. You know I'm tryin' to go play ball after school, and you put that dro in my backpack. I wasn't goin' out like that."

Carlos talked louder as the memory of that school day came rushing back to him. Two years ago, the school cop had done a random bag check in the hallway and found dro in his pack. Carlos was dragged out of P.E. and hauled into the principal's office. He told the principal that it wasn't his, but he knew who it belonged to. He just needed until the closing school bell to get the person to confess.

Against her better judgment, the principal accepted the arrangement. Carlos was always persuasive. At lunch, Robert had tapped him on the shoulder and said that he appreciated the cover. Carlos then told him he wasn't covering anything and Robert had until the end of the day to turn himself in.

He didn't believe Carlos would turn him in, but Robert found out differently. At the end of the day, Carlos went to the principal's office and explained the situation. She verified his story using the surveillance cameras in the hallway, and Robert was carted off to juvie.

Robert then spent the next 20 months plotting his revenge on Carlos. In the meantime, he missed Halloween—his favorite holiday, because he got to dress up, and more importantly, collect candy from all the "good candy neighborhoods." For that one day, being small paid off, and he fit in with the other kids. And for that one day of the year...he belonged.

"No," said Carlos as he lowered his hands. "You tried to get me in trouble. I wasn't about to take the fall for you. Tryin' to get up outta here. Just like you, bruh," Carlos reached for Robert's arm and tried to wrestle the gun away from him.

He had at least 50 pounds on Robert, and it should have been a no-contest. But Robert was bound and determined to make Carlos pay. The two struggled. Carlos tripped over the curbside, and Robert got control of the gun.

Sonny rushed forward.

Bang. Bang. Bang.

The smell of gunpowder filled the air and the school children's lungs. Sonny caught Carlos as his body slid to the ground. His eyes were still open, and Sonny begged him to hold on. Help was coming.

But Carlos went limp. And Sonny's best friend was ripped away.

* * *

That night, as Sonny got ready for bed, he noticed a hole in the right sleeve of his black hoodie. So he interrupted Constance's bedtime prayer to show it to her.

Constance had already rolled back the corner of her floral duvet and was kneeling by her bedside. She was minutes away from being sound asleep when Sonny opened the door without knocking and walked in.

"Granny, I gotta hole in my sweatshirt," he held his head to the side and waited for Constance to inspect the damage.

Constance looked at Sonny irritated at the interruption, but as he joined her on the floor, she ran her thumb around the hole and immediately noticed its burnt crisp edges. She'd seen this type of hole before—when Victor Junior's clothes were returned to her after his murder.

"Sonny," Constance said as she looked up slowly, "this is a bullet hole." She sighed and let the weight of her words sink in.

"A bullet hole?" his nose wrinkled. "Wha-d'ya mean?"

Constance flung her prayer journal on the bed and got up slowly from her kneeling position, then peered into his eyes. "Sonny. You were shot."

He sank down on the edge of the bed and began to replay those last seconds with Carlos in his head. He couldn't remember any blood. He didn't remember any pain. Nothing made sense. Granny was overreacting.

"Hmm. Guess I was lucky then," he finally said.

Constance's blood boiled, and she swatted Sonny's left ear. How could he be so stupid? she wondered. He definitely hadn't inherited her brains, or even Victor Junior's brains. This was logic (or the lack thereof) that could've only come from Victor Senior's side of the family.

"Sonny Jackson! You were *not* lucky. Luck had nothing to do with it. It was the hand of the Almighty that spared you today, and you need to learn to give credit where credit is due."

"S-sorry, Granny," Sonny rubbed his ear. "I was just talking."

"That's your problem. You just talk. You just do. You just hang around with whoever with no thought to the consequences. Luck refers to favor from Lucifer—the devil!" Constance paced back and forth, trying to keep her voice steady.

"Don't you understand? Lucifer—the devil—wants your life snuffed out...just like he snuffed out your father's," Constance snapped her fingers for emphasis. "And *he* has absolutely nothing to do with your heart still beating in your chest at this moment."

Sitting on the edge of the bed, Sonny looked down at his shoes.

This is just a coincidence—that there's a hole in my sweatshirt. Granny's always blowin' things out the water.

"Sonny," Constance tried to choke back the emotion, "I just don't know how many more chances Providence is going to give." Her voice cracked as she lowered herself back to her knees and continued to pray for him...as she did every night.

* * *

For the next three weeks, Sonny wore a gray hooded sweatshirt with the phrase "RIP Carlos" airbrushed, along with a picture of him, on the front. Most days, he lost the drive to play ball. Just reminded him that Carlos wasn't around anymore.

A few months after Carlos's death, Sonny decided it was time to get something more permanent than a sweatshirt to remember him by. And Constance was too tired to fight him on the matter.

CHAPTER TWENTY-FIVE

The bell on the Music City Tattoo Culture door clanged as Sonny swung it open, and the waiting room was filled with the constant buzz of a tattoo gun. As Sonny approached the front desk, he handed the signed permission slip to the attendant.

Sonny wasn't interested in looking at the images of the tattoo art that hung on the wall. He already knew what his ink would say—*R.I.P. Carlos 3-10-00.*

After he took a seat, though, he bit his lip as the smell of burning skin began to affect his usually stable stomach. Something felt off, and for a moment, he had second thoughts. Then he had to remind himself why he was getting this tattoo.

To begin with, he and Los had always talked about getting tatted together. But now that he was gone, it seemed right that his first tattoo forever link him to his best friend. Carlos was a part of his story, and a tattoo would help keep his memory alive.

Twenty minutes later, he sat in a chair that looked just like the one he sat on when at the orthodontist. The bearded tattoo artist asked him to pick out his *Rest-In-Peace* emblem that he would place next to Carlos's name and date of death.

Sonny pointed. The artist nodded and snapped on his surgical gloves, then rubbed Sonny's arm hard with alcohol.

Sonny took a deep breath as the needle began to pierce his skin. The pain felt good, and the hurt he'd been holding on to since Carlos had left seemed to escape through his pores.

An hour later, the artist nudged Sonny on the shoulder, and he snapped to attention. He looked at his reddish and green swollen arm and then smiled. Carlos would be a part of him forever now.

But he still felt something was missing.

CHAPTER TWENTY-SIX

Constance sat in her rocking chair, and once again, relived happy moments from her childhood. They were clear now; the years of sadness had been washed away with her visit to Wharton last Spring. She could almost smell the strong coffee brewing in the kitchen and hear the sound of bacon sizzling in the cast-iron skillet, seasoned with the goodness of being used for more than a generation.

Then she thought again of the first day she had arrived on campus, after the long bus ride across the plains of Texas, the Ozarks of Arkansas, and into the hills of Tennessee. She had been filled with so much promise and hope for the future.

The full scholarship had made a way out of no way for her to go to college, and she had been determined to change her family tree and bring honor and respect to her parents. Then came Victor Senior. But she wasn't bitter anymore. He did bring her the joy of Victor Junior, and now, the years of pain and suffering seemed to have a purpose.

But Sonny appeared to be on the same path as her sweet baby, Victor Junior. He hardly came home. And ran the streets until all hours of the night—ever since Carlos had been murdered. Carlos was to Sonny, what Rachel had been to Victor Junior. And Constance simply could not bear to see the cycle repeat itself.

"No, Lord, I've done all that I can do," Constance said in a low whisper, her rocking chair slowed to a stop. Her chin rested on her chest, and her hand fell limp to her side. And she stayed that way until Sonny found her the next morning.

She had left him without saying good-bye, just like everyone else.

* * *

Flower arrangements filled the altar area at the front of Buchanan. Word of Constance's passing spread quickly to her classmates and former students, and wreaths and cards from all over the country were displayed.

Guests arrived two hours early so they could find a seat inside the sanctuary, and every seat was filled. Except for the front row reserved for family. Sonny sat there alone in his black suit and tie.

After the sanctuary cleared out, Sonny sat there and stared at the brown casket. Neither Rachel nor Coach Grimes had bothered to show up.

I'm with you, Sonny thought he heard.

No one else cares. You're on your own.

Sonny clenched his fist and punched at the padded pew. She had left him. She had left him all by himself. Just like everyone else.

What's going to happen to me now?

Sonny felt a tap on his shoulder and turned to see Paige sitting on the pew behind him.

She leaned forward and whispered, "I'm sorry about your granny."

Sonny nodded and tried to push Constance out of his mind. "Was gonna happen sooner or later."

"Sonny, my parents said you can come live with us. They want to adopt you, too." Paige's eyes were shining, and she talked fast. "We could be brother and sister, for real. Go to school together. We even have a swimming pool, and you could…"

They'll leave you too.

"I'm not leavin', Paige."

"What do you mean? There's nothing here…"

"I'm here! I've been here. Everyone else has left, but I'm not…"

"Sonny, who's gonna take care of you? You need…"

"I don't need nobody but myself. I got everything I need," Sonny looked down at the palms of his hands and nodded his head. From now on, it was just him, and he wasn't pinning his hope on nothing or no one.

"Sonny, please just come stay with us for a little while. My parents are really nice," Paige pointed to her parents standing at the back of the church. They both stood with fake smiles pasted on their faces, holding hands like some suckers.

"Nah. I'm good."

Paige sniffed and wiped a tear from her cheek. She sat there and tried to think of a different way to convince him to come live with them. He was alone in the world, and her parents were offering him a way out. *Why don't he just take it?*

"I gotta go," Sonny said impatiently.

"Oh, okay. Can we give you a ride home? My parents won't mind."

"Nah. I just need to be alone." Sonny got up from his pew and forced a smile at Paige. "I'm good. I promise."

Paige leaned in for a hug, and Sonny patted her on the back.

"See ya later."

Paige hoped he meant it.

CHAPTER TWENTY-SEVEN

The basketball court became Sonny's sanctuary. There, he could quiet the voices and prove everyone wrong. The night of Constance's funeral, the gym was dimly lit, and the lights at the edge of the court flickered. The floor felt grimy from last night's game, and bits of stale popcorn and potato chip bags were strewn throughout the bleachers.

Only people with no respect for the game leave trash.

He hated those people.

He ran back to the baseline and did four more sets of suicides.

His Adidas's squeaked like bad breaks as he touched the baseline and pivoted. It was his eighth set of full-court suicides. The sweat running down his forehead mixed in with the tears running down his cheeks.

He paused to wipe his face with the corner of his faded gray t-shirt that read, *Just Do It*, and scratched at his arm absentmindedly.

How could she leave me? And what's gonna happen to me now?

Constance had been the center of Sonny's life for the past eleven years. She'd rescued him when his mother was too strung out on drugs to change his diaper. She'd taken him to school and read him bedtime stories. When he had memories of his dad and couldn't sleep, Constance sat in the rocking chair all night and hummed hymns until the voices quieted.

But he had to forget about her. It was just him now.

Sonny lined up in a sprinter's stance and leaned forward. The floor didn't look like it'd been mopped since the Celtics won the NBA championship, so it didn't matter if his sweat added to the sweat of others. He took off and smacked every dirty black and red line with the anger he felt gripping his heart.

Sonny slumped to the floor, took a deep breath, and tried not to let his face touch the floor. He wanted to forget the black suit and tie hanging out of his gym bag. He tried to force the images of life with her out of his head. It was just him now.

* * *

Members from Buchanan stayed with Sonny a few days at a time, until a social worker came for him and his things. He left without a fight and sat in the back seat as he was carted off to a foster home and away from everything he'd known and everything his granny had given.

CHAPTER TWENTY-EIGHT

Reesha Perkins was a career-foster parent. She was stable. Well, stable enough for DHS and to qualify as a foster parent. She hadn't moved in more than three years. All three of her children went to school most days, and her happiness came in the mail on the 1st and 15th of the month, when her checks arrived.

Reesha, Sonny's assigned foster mom, parked her silver SUV in the handicapped spot in front of Young's Market, even though her handicapped sticker had expired. She dug into her oversized, Gucci knock-off handbag to fish out $4.17. She knew exactly how much a loaf of white bread, a bag of sour-cream potato chips, and a bottle of orange soda cost. Because she bought the same thing every three or four days. She had trouble holding the change in her inch-long, leopard-print fingernails but was relieved she didn't have to get out of the car this time.

"Get a loaf of bread, some chips, and Orange Faygo. Don't get that off-brand soda—it taste like sugar water," Reesha pressed the exact change in Sonny's hand. "Buy you something to eat too."

Sonny slid out of the passenger's seat and slammed the Suburban door a little harder than necessary. It was her prized possession, so he slammed the door to spite her.

"Welcome to Young's Market," Mr. Young said in his thick Korean accent from behind the bullet-proof glass window. He stayed behind the glass after dark nowadays and watched the black and blue surveillance monitors.

Sonny made eye contact with Mr. Young and nodded. He didn't have time to waste words on Mr. Young. A minute later, he picked up the dinner items for Reesha's daughter and headed to the frozen food aisle. As he looked through the smudged glass at the Hungry-Man fried-chicken dinner, he remembered the smell of Constance's fried chicken on

Sunday afternoons. After church, she would always say, "Sonny, what would you like for Sunday dinner?"

"Uhhh, fried chicken, mashed potatoes..."

"...collard greens and apple pie," Constance finished with her hands on her hips.

"Yes, ma'am," answered Sonny as he got up to wrap his arms around her waist.

"Get out of my kitchen, boy. I need to get started on Sunday dinner," she would say as she tried to swat him with her wooden kitchen spoon. But Sonny always knew what was coming and ducked out of her reach just in time.

He missed those Sunday afternoons—the sounds of Sam Cooke singing in the kitchen and the smells that wafted all through the house. No one else could make friend chicken like Granny.

He snapped back to reality at the sound of Reesha's voice.

"Sonny, what is takin' you so long, boy? You know, I got to be home to watch *Living Single*. Dang, you can't do nothin' right," Reesha tried to snatch the requested items out of his hands. "Gimme my money back," she snapped her fingers.

Sonny handed over the bread, chips, and soda. Then he grabbed a Hungry-Man salisbury steak out of the freezer and lumbered behind Reesha to the checkout aisle where she handed her items to Mr. Young.

"Will this be all, ma'am?" Mr. Young asked as he let his gaze fall on Sonny with his blue box clenched to his chest.

"Nah, we separate," Reesha said. Mr. Young rang up the purchases and announced the total.

"Four dollars, seventeen cents, please."

Reesha dropped the exact change on the counter and grabbed the plastic bag full of tonight's "nutrition-rich" dinner.

"Thank you very much," Mr. Young gave a polite nod as he unrumpled the dollar bills and placed them in the register.

Sonny put his salisbury steak on the counter and looked at Mr. Young. The owner recognized Sonny from three years ago, and he was almost sure what Mr. Young was thinking. He began to shift his weight back and forth on his feet and tried to come up with something to say.

"Your dinner free tonight. I know pain of hunger, and I forgive you for stealing," a smile spread across Mr. Young's face as he took Sonny's dinner and carefully placed it in a plastic bag. Then he handed it to him along with a refrigerator magnet that read "Jesus Loves You—The Nashville Christian Korean Church."

Sonny cocked his head to the side and tried to read whether or not Mr. Young was being serious. No one had been this kind to him since his granny died.

Mr. Young smiled and nodded.

"Th-thanks," Sonny said as he picked up the dinner and put down the magnet. He quickened his pace as he got closer to the door. He didn't want to give Mr. Young a chance to change his mind.

"'Bout time," said Reesha as she let out a "tsk." "You almost got left, boy."

Sonny just sat in the vehicle and didn't make eye contact. He'd gotten used to blocking out the world.

* * *

Sonny couldn't wait for his senior year of high school to start. The head dancer, Leslie, would be the highlight. All last year, he'd been try-ing to get her to notice him. Occasionally, she'd smiled at him from the sideline when he had made a good shot. But she had never really acknowledged him off the court.

Sonny thought, Leslie was the prettiest girl in school, with hazel green eyes and jet black hair that hung down to her waist. All the guys had been trying to get with her—from the very first day she darkened the doors of East High school as a freshman. But Sonny made it a point to do things differently—he'd tried to make her laugh every time they were in earshot of each other.

He was hoping that his good sense of humor and being the best play-er on the basketball team would help her overlook his acne and ears that were too big for his head. He was pretty sure if he could just get with Leslie, everything in his life would be okay.

CHAPTER TWENTY-NINE

S onny drove through the James Cayce Homes roundabout just above the speed limit. He slowed down a bit for the speed bumps, but he liked the sound of his Chevy Impala. He also liked the way people looked up when they heard Bone Thugs-N-Harmony banging out his trunk.

He was on his way to pick up Leslie so they could go to the movies. It was a breezy Saturday afternoon, and the neighbors were sitting outside on their stoops. Most of them were smoking, drinking, or playing cards as he pulled up to the front of her red-brick building, next to the dirt front yard.

Sonny honked twice, and within seconds, Leslie looked out her bedroom window and waved. They'd been going together for a few months, and he knew she'd be down in a minute.

In his mind, they were meant to be together. She was a dancer, and he was a ball player. She was short, like her Mexican mother, but athletic like her Black dad. She had the best of both worlds—curly hair and a face and spirit that reminded him of his granny.

She was *always* trying to take care of him, and he liked the way that Leslie cared. No one had really made a fuss over him since his grandmother died, and it was good to have that feeling again—that someone would notice if you didn't eat or didn't brush your teeth... or whatever.

Leslie skipped down the steps outside her apartment. She was wearing a white halter top that showed her belly button, her hair pushed up in a high ponytail with a butterfly clip. Knowing that she was headed for him made Sonny's chest swell, especially when he noticed that the men standing around were focused on her booty as she walked by.

"Hey, babe," Leslie said as she slid into the car and leaned over to give Sonny a kiss.

Sonny gave her butt a squeeze and kept one eye open as he kissed her back, flashing a thumbs-up to the guys on one of the stoops.

"Babe, I've got something to tell you," Leslie smiled and said in a sing-song way.

"Okay. What's up?" Sonny said.

"I just wanted to say that you are now stuck with me for life," Leslie squeezed Sonny's shoulder and patted his cheek.

Sonny tilted his head to the side and pressed his lips together. "Les... umm...could you explain that a bit more?"

"Well, last week my mom took me to the doctor because I was feeling sick. Remember, I missed a couple days of school? The doctor said...I'm six weeks pregnant!"

"Pregnant...huh?" Sonny stared straight ahead as he pulled at the goatee hairs on his chin. He knew he'd be a dad at some point. But he'd never thought about what the moment would feel like when he found out.

The thing is, he didn't feel anything. He just sat there in the car rubbing his chin. Leslie patted him on the hand and tried to get him to look at her.

"Yep. Pregnant. It's going to be me and you from now on, Sonny. What do you think we should call the baby? Do you think it'll be a boy or a girl? Do twins run in your family?" Leslie went on non-stop for the next few minutes, talking about them and about the baby.

Sonny wasn't sure what to say. At least, if he was having a baby with Leslie, it would be a cute baby, because both of them had good hair and straight teeth.

"So, what you wanna see?" he shifted the car into drive, and they headed toward the movies.

"You know, this is how my mom hooked my dad," Leslie still wasn't finished with the baby subject, "and they've been together 20 years. So it's only natural that the same thing would happen to me. But I'm happy it's happening with you." She looked over at him and smiled.

"Anyway...I don't know. You pick. But you have to buy me double the movie snacks, because I'm eating for at least two now," Leslie rubbed her stomach and leaned back in the passenger seat.

* * *

Every few minutes, Sonny scanned the crowd for Rachel. She said she was coming to the game to see him play. But she'd said stuff like that before. For some reason, he believed her this time. Something in her voice had been different.

With two seconds on the clock, Coach Grimes called a time-out. The Lions needed this win to make it to the playoffs, and they were down by three against their rival—Harding.

Jontae inbounded to Sonny, and Sonny looked down at the 3-point line, closed his eyes, and took the shot. Then he opened them back up just in time to see the ball swish through the net. And the crowd erupted.

He had tied the game with his eyes closed.

This was a good night. The crowd was a little bit louder. The lights were a little bit brighter. And every Lion in the gym seemed to be clapping and jumping. Then he heard Rachel's voice above all the rest. Hollering like she'd been to every single game of his life.

"That's *my* son! That's *my* son!" The pride in her voice swelled, and her eyes had cleared. It felt good to have *someone* cheering for him. Sonny pointed to her and waved.

The Lions beat Harding in overtime, and Rachel waited for Sonny after the game.

As she paced back and forth, she kept her eye on the locker room exit. Rachel hadn't seen Sonny in five years, since the incident on the sidewalk, and she was worried he hadn't forgotten about it.

Out there on the court tonight, he had looked just like Victor Junior. She touched the butterfly necklace as she remembered Sonny's father. It seemed like it'd been a lifetime since he had left. How she wished he could have stayed. Her life would have been so different. But he had let himself get killed. And now she was a single 33-year-old mother of three...each with a different dad.

She was determined to keep this baby, though. And she couldn't wait to tell Sonny that she was clean, had a job, and he could come and live with her soon.

The door opened, and Sonny walked out of the locker room and slowly up to Rachel. He adjusted the strap on his gym bag and looked her over. There was something going on, but he couldn't tell just what. She looked better. She had dressed her age and had gained some weight. And on top of that, the bruises on her arms had almost faded.

"Hey, you," she called out. "You looked good out there tonight. Reminded me of your father."

Coach Grimes had said the same thing to him last week—that he played with the same fire as his dad. He nodded and shifted from one foot to the other as Rachel looked him over.

"You look just like him, Sonny. I miss him, you know," her voice trailed off, and her gaze momentarily faded into the past. "Hey, I'm sorry I didn't come to Constance's funeral. She never really liked me. So I thought it'd be best if I stayed away."

"It's cool," Sonny said as he remembered sitting on the front pew completely alone. He thought about telling Rachel she was going to be a grandmother, but she interrupted his thoughts first.

"I'm having another baby. A boy. I hope he's just like you," Rachel sounded upbeat and Sonny wondered why. "I'm gonna get my life together, okay?" she paused and searched his eyes. "I'm really gonna pull everything together so that you and Paige, and me and this new baby can be a family. A real one."

He stood there in silence and let his gaze pierce Rachel's heart. He'd heard all this before. The promises to get it together and come back for him. But she had always managed to come up short.

No, he wouldn't give her any hope. In six months, he'd be out of the system and on his own. After that, he wouldn't need anyone else but himself.

Rachel leaned in for a hug, and Sonny leaned just out of reach, ending the conversation. "Okay, Ma. Catch up with ya later."

Reesha, his foster mother, was probably waiting for him outside. She'd left him stranded before when he ran late, and he didn't feel like walking home tonight.

CHAPTER THIRTY

Sonny limped into the East High School cafeteria and made his way toward the lunch line. He leaned one of his crutches against the stainless-steel rail, then tried to pick up a lunch tray and stay balanced. His other crutch crashed to the ground, and he looked toward the emergency exit sign. Maybe coming in here was a bad idea.

"Let me help you with that, babe," Leslie rested her hand on his lower back and leaned down to pick up his crutch. "Why don't you go have a seat? I'll get your food for you."

"You're always right on time."

"Yeah, what would you do without me?"

"I'd be a-ight." A lump filled his throat.

You don't need anybody.

"Whatever, boy. Go sit down."

Sonny adjusted himself on his crutches and headed toward a table filled with his teammates. He didn't need her, but it was nice to have her around. She admired everything he did. Right or wrong.

"What's up, man? How you been?" Jontae stood up from the table and let Sonny have the seat near the edge.

"Just tryin' to get better. It's not lookin' good, though."

"What did the doc say?"

"Torn ACL."

"Awhhh man. You out for the season?"

"Yeah."

"You'll be able to still play though, eventually, right?" Jontae asked.

"Depends on how it heals after surgery. Could be out for good, cuz."

"Man, that's messed up."

Sonny nodded and thought about what he would do without basketball. It was the sole constant in his life. What would he be without it? Leslie slid his tray in front of him and smiled.

"Need anything else?" she asked.

"Nah, I'm good."

"Sure thing. See you after school?"

"Not sure."

"Why? You ain't got nowhere to be," Leslie's eyebrows knit together.

"Look, I said I'm not sure. Just leave it."

"What's your problem? You all in my face when you need somethin'. Then when I want to hang out, you start actin' brand-new."

"Les, I'm not trying to get into all that right now," Sonny looked up from his lunch tray and motioned for her to leave.

"It's cool, Negro. You know what? Your sorry tail is gonna need me for somethin'. And when you do, forget my name. Because I'm tired of dealin' with your back-and-forth. Either you want me, or you don't. Call me when you've made up your mind for good."

Sonny stared into the distance and waited for Leslie to finish her rant. "Are you done?"

Leslie gasped and turned to walk toward the exit. Two seconds later, she marched back to Sonny and dumped his lunch tray on his lap. Applause erupted from the next table over, and the girls sitting there whooped and hollered.

"Yeah...now I'm done."

Chapter Thirty-One

"Sonny Jackson?" A chubby lady with a clipboard scanned the waiting room to see if the name registered with anyone. Slowly, Sonny stood up and slung the strap of his gym bag over his shoulder. The day of emancipation had come. So why didn't he feel like he had anything to look forward to?

"Yeah. That's me," Sonny nodded and held up two fingers. The woman looked at him over her white-rimmed glasses and nodded her head.

"Follow me, Mr. Jackson." She led him down a long corridor, up a flight of stairs, and around the corner to an office with seven or eight desks. The room was decorated with skinny fake plants that needed to be dusted in each of the corners.

Scanning the room, Sonny noticed that all the staff seemed to be buried in their own world of papers and file folders. Then he noticed the chubby lady pointing him to a desk in the far left corner.

"Ms. Rickson is over there."

Sonny nodded and took a deep breath. This was it. He shuffled through the desks, not making eye contact with anyone. He'd been looking forward to this day for a long time, but now that it was here, he wasn't sure what would happen next.

Ms. Rickson looked up from her desk. "Sonny Jackson?"

"Yes, ma'am."

"Have a seat, please."

Sonny placed his gym bag on the floor and sat in the chair across from her.

"So, congrats on turning 18," Ms. Rickson stared at the manila folder in front of her. "It's a huge milestone."

He nodded and pulled on his pant leg.

"Okay, so you have a couple of options now that you've *aged out* of the system. We like kids who have turned 18 to stay connected, but the program is totally voluntary. You've been in a group home for almost a year, but we could try to match you with one of the private living arrangements and get you additional support until you turn 21."

Sonny thought about the past three years and of the foster and group homes he'd been bounced in and out of. Then there were the Sunday play-dates when parents wanting to adopt came to look at the children, always heading for the babies first.

Even when he did get placed with a family, it never lasted long. And once he started to get hair on his face—that was the end of his chance for real parents. No, he would not open up himself to be turned away again. He'd figure it out on his own. He'd gotten himself this far.

"Nah. I'm good," he shook his head, rejecting her offer.

Ms. Rickson's eyebrows lifted, and she made some notes on his file. "Okay, there is one more option. If you stay in school, we'll give you $1,256 per month until you graduate. That'll only give you a couple of months, but it's better than nothing."

Sonny nodded.

Finally, he would be on his own. He could make his own choices. Buy his own food. And never have to worry about being sent away again. *Then again,* he thought, *where am I gonna go? And where am I gonna sleep?*

"Okay, so you need to check in with us monthly. To let me know how you're doing."

He nodded and took the card that Ms. Rickson handed him.

"Make sure you don't forget your monthly appointments and be sure to send in your report cards as proof of enrollment. Any questions?"

Sonny moved to stand up. "Nah. I'm good," he said again. He thought about how long he'd wished for this moment. He picked up his gym bag and headed back down the stairs. That was it. He was free.

But free to do what?

Sonny shoved the debit card Ms. Rickson had given him in his pocket and headed out to his car. It felt good to have so much money in his pocket, but also weird, because he didn't know where to begin.

Just then, his stomach started to rumble. Food. That was always a good start. He decided to celebrate "aging out" with some Prince's.

* * *

Sonny lined up on the sidewalk with the other 20-or-so people standing in line for Prince's Hot Chicken. The mom-and-pop store front had been a staple for 60 years—serving mostly the after-club crowd until the wee hours of the morning. But only now, after so many white people had discovered hot chicken, did he have to wait in line on the sidewalk during the middle of the day.

Sonny used to be able to go inside and get a seat at a table with a sticky tablecloth in under five minutes. But that wasn't the case anymore. As the smell of Tabasco sauce and hot chicken grease eased out to the sidewalk, he already decided he would get the extra hot sandwich. He was in a melt-your-face kind of mood, and Prince's would do the trick.

In the meantime, he had nothing to do but focus on the dandruff in the hair of the lady in front of him. She was short, and he could look straight down onto the crown of her head. The dandruff was nasty, and he couldn't understand why she didn't take better care of her hair. He put his hands in his pockets and took a deep breath. It would be a long wait, but he wasn't in a hurry anyway.

He took the copy of the slimy menu the lady with the dandruff handed him and passed it to the person behind. He didn't need to look at it. Then he decided he would get Leslie the mild since she was pregnant.

"Sonny! Sonny Jackson, is that you?" said a short round girl with a hairnet and grease stains on her blue apron.

Sonny recognized the voice but couldn't place the face. He just sort of squinted and kept looking straight ahead without acknowledging he knew the woman.

"Sonny, do you remember me? It's me—Colleen." The girl made her way through the line and tapped Sonny on the arm. His shoulder was out of reach.

Colleen? Colleen? The name didn't ring a bell. And neither did her body. *Where could I know her from?* Sonny gave Colleen a half-smile and looked down at the crack in the pavement.

"You, Carlos, and me were in the seventh grade together. Remember?"

Sonny nodded slowly as he thought about Carlos and himself in the seventh grade. They had gotten into so much trouble that year, snapping girls' bra straps, skipping music class, stealing Jello from the cafeteria, and quitting school for all of two weeks. Good times.

"Y'all bought me brand-new Tommy shirts when the kids at school were making fun of me wearing the same shirt every day," Colleen said as she leaned forward to squeeze Sonny's forearm.

He flexed his arm muscle just to let her know he was all man. Colleen had a crush on Sonny during middle school, and it seemed the flame was still flickering.

"Yeah," Sonny said with a slight grin. "I remember that." He ran his hands through his brown curls and remembered how he and Carlos had boosted those Tommy shirts from the Arcade. He had told Carlos what was goin' on with Colleen, and they decided they'd help her out.

"I never forgot what y'all did for me," Colleen slipped off her hairnet and took off her apron. The years had been good to Colleen. Her skin wasn't blotchy anymore, and she had picked up some weight in the right places.

"Hey, I'm about to take a lunch break. Come inside with me," Colleen slipped her arm around his waist.

Sonny nodded and let his steps fall in line with hers. She pointed him to a booth marked "Employees Only" and told him to wait there. Then she was back in 20 minutes with trays full of enough food to last three days. Sonny smiled and picked up the plate closest to him.

What about Leslie?

After lunch, they exchanged numbers. From then on, all Sonny could think about was how everything else had faded to gray when talking to Colleen. She had smiled at him. Rubbed his hand. And laughed at everything he said.

But Sonny went home to Leslie. And to her pregnancy. She was hot. She was cold. She wanted pickles. She wanted peanut butter. She made him clean the house because her back hurt. She sent him to buy groceries even though she wasn't cooking much anymore. And every time she called his name, Sonny clenched his jaw and braced for the next order. Peace and quiet came only when she slept.

* * *

Sonny lay on Leslie's sectional sofa and tried to ignore the pain in his chest. He just couldn't accept that he was going to have to take care of another person. Leslie herself was demanding so much. She'd shown him her registry list yesterday, along with the costs. But everything he owned was folded and stacked in three neat piles in his gym bag. He wanted to swallow, but his mouth was too dry. He thought about what Reesha had told him over and over again, sometimes while digging her nails into his arms—*You ain't got nothin', and you ain't never gonna be nothin'.* He knew now that she was right.

They'd be better off without you.

Sonny reached for his phone and texted Colleen. She answered back in seconds. She had been showing up in his dreams since they'd had lunch. He slid his feet into his tennis shoes and crept back to the bedroom to check on Leslie.

She was sound asleep.

Grabbing his keys from the kitchen counter, Sonny slung his gym bag over his shoulder and locked the door on his way out. *It's better this way,* he thought, and shoved the key in the ignition of his Impala.

* * *

Six months after Sonny moved in with Colleen, she put him out. She worked two jobs, went to school, and kept a pristine house. All Sonny wanted to do all day was lay around the house and occasionally go to Hartman and play ball.

But she wasn't down for supporting anyone else but herself. So she told Sonny he had two weeks to get a job or he could leave.

He left.

Then a friend told him that Leslie had the baby…a girl. So he gave her a call and asked if he could come and see her.

He wasn't surprised when she said yes.

CHAPTER THIRTY-TWO

The Air Jordan display took up an entire wall of the Foot Locker, and the Jumpman logo greeted the customers as they walked in the door. Most were drawn by the idea of being "like Mike." Sonny picked up the white shoe with gray elephant skin around the toe and heel. Constance had bought him his first pair of Jordans just like these.

He turned the shoe over in his hand and remembered what it had been like to walk down the street the first day he'd worn them. There was nothing like being on the block in a fresh pair of J's.

"Y'all got these in an 11?" Sonny said to the nearest sales person.

"Let me go to the back and check."

He handed the display shoe to the person and stuck his hands in his pockets, then focused on the shelves of shoes in front of him, stacked almost to the ceiling. The newer Jordans had too many colors and looked fake. He preferred the classic black, white, gray, and red. More colors than that were just extra and too hard to match.

As the sales associate returned, Sonny took a seat on the bench.

"Didn't have an 11. But we had a 10 and a 12. So I got you both."

"Alright." He slid off his shoes and hoped no weird smells escaped. He looked up at the sales associate's face but didn't notice any changes. Deciding he must be good, he lifted the lid of the Air Jordan shoebox and took in a deep breath. Nothing compared to the smell of fresh kicks.

He pushed the tissue paper aside and lifted out the right shoe, adjusted the shoelaces and tongue, and slid in his foot. Although the Jordan hugged his foot a little too tight, he ignored the feeling and put on the left shoe. Then he stood up and walked toward the mirror next to the display.

He felt ten feet tall, and the girl with brown eyes, trying on running shoes, smiled at him. As he walked up and down the aisle, the sales associate leaned on the clothing rack with his head in the crook of his elbow and waited.

Constance had started this craze without even knowing it. She didn't know anything about Jordans. She had just gone to the store and asked for the best pair of basketball shoes there. Sonny's mouth had fallen wide open when his granny gave them to him on the day of his first basketball game. She was so happy that he was happy. Even now, Sonny couldn't believe she'd gotten him Jordans.

He had planned to wear them in the first game, but that was before one of his teammates advised him against it. "Man. Can't nobody see 'em if you wear 'em in the game. You need to wear those to school." Sonny took his advice and wore his Adidas's instead. Now, his baby would have her first pair of J's too.

He realized that he had forgotten the whole reason he'd come into the store...to get Sonya her first pair of J's. He looked down at the AJ III's on his feet and decided that they were too small anyway. So he went back to the bench and shoved the shoes into the box. He didn't bother to straighten the tissue paper.

"Where are the baby Jordans?" Sonny looked at the associate.

"Did these work for you?"

"Nah. Too small."

"I could order one size up and have them shipped to your house."

"Nah. I'm good," Sonny scanned the perimeter of the store and saw the kids' section marked at the far right corner. He slid his feet back into his shoes and headed to the back to pick out a pair of baby shoes for his girl.

There weren't many choices. After scanning the wall, he found three pair. One with a pink Jumpman logo. *Seriously?* A pair of soft bottoms that looked more like socks than shoes. *Absolutely not.* And a pair of red and black classics. *These will have to do.* He didn't know the baby's shoe size, but these were the smallest pair they had. If anything, Sonya could grow into them.

He headed to the register and pulled out the four 20's in his pocket.

"Did you find everything okay today?" the woman behind the register smiled as she scanned the baby shoes and slid them in an oversized Footlocker bag.

"Uh-huh."

"Would you like to protect your shoes from rain, snow, and leather damage with weather protectant?"

Sonny looked at her for a minute and tilted to his head to the side. Someone was always looking for a come-up. *Weather protectant for baby shoes?* "Nah. I won't be needin' that."

"Well, if you change your mind, you can pick it up anytime," she pushed a few more buttons on the register. "Your total is $56.32."

Sonny slid over three of his four 20's and shoved the last one in his pocket. He smiled as he thought about how Sonya would look in her little Jordans. She probably had a red bib or something to match. He'd get her a jumper with a matching logo when he got her the next pair.

The cashier handed him his change along with his bag. Sonny walked out, relieved that he had something to give his daughter.

* * *

He parked his burgundy car in the gravel driveway in front of Leslie's side of the duplex and knocked gently, peering through the sagging screen door. Leslie's hair was pulled up high on her head, and her gold hoop earrings framed her face. Sonny thought she looked the same as always.

Leslie opened the screen door and pressed her lips together in a straight line to keep from smiling. "Let me introduce you to your daughter," she turned to the playpen to pick up a baby girl with fat little legs and a pink bow in her hair.

At first, Sonny held the baby awkwardly at arm's length and looked at her as if she might poop at any moment. Then he looked at Leslie and then back at the baby. Yeah, the baby looked more like Leslie, but she had his sharp nose and cleft chin. It was his all right.

After handing the baby back to Leslie, he moved the unfolded laundry over to make a place for himself on the sofa. "You got anything to eat?"

Leslie laughed and moved quickly toward the kitchen. Sonny reminded her of her dad, always hungry and looking for something to eat. Her mother had told her many times, "The only way to keep a man is to keep him fed." And Leslie was determined not to make Sonny leave her again.

"If you give me a couple of hours, I can make enchiladas."

"All right. I ain't got nowhere to be."

Leslie had her family back, and she was determined to make it work this time. She would do anything Sonny asked to keep him happy and to keep their family together.

Two hours later, Leslie brought Sonny a plate of enchiladas and re-fried beans and sat it down in front of him on the coffee table. Sonny didn't look up from the basketball game. "Got any soda?"

"Coming right up."

Sonny needed her, and all was right with the world again.

Chapter Thirty-Three

P aige leaned against the rail at the bottom of the steps in front of the Davidson County Courthouse and waited for Sonny to come outside. She had a class that started in 30 minutes, and naturally, he was taking his sweet time.

She looked at her watch again and thought about how many times she'd been to this courthouse. This morning, she didn't even have to stop and ask the officer at the front desk for directions. She knew exactly where she was going and what to do. And it was such a waste of her time.

Finally. Paige looked up when she heard Sonny clear his throat. She saw him zip up the jacket that she had borrowed for him earlier this morning from her dad, and he walked down the steps slowly. "Thanks," he said as he shoved his hands in his pockets and kicked at the edge of the steps.

"Look, Sonny, I can't keep using my tuition money to bail you out. My parents are going to wonder why I can't pay my rent."

"Least you got somebody to worry about you."

"Don't you start that again! You could have had the same thing, but…"

Sonny held up his hand and nodded, "I get it. You're a college kid, and you got responsibilities. I won't trouble you anymore."

Paige exhaled and rubbed her temples. "It's not that. You're not any trouble. It's just…I want you to do better. I want you to *be* better."

"This is the only way I know to be," he pounded his hands on his chest and stooped down to make eye contact with her. "I been on my own since 15. Fifteen, Paige. Ain't nobody ever looked out for me. I didn't get to grow up on a cul-de-sac with my parents tucking me in, kissing me goodnight, and wishing me sweet dreams."

"I know. I know."

"You don't know! You don't know what it's like to not know where you're gonna sleep at night. You don't know what it's like to count the hours 'til the library is open, so you can wash up and use the bathroom in a decent place. You don't know what it's like to steal a cell phone from a mom sitting at Starbucks feeding her baby, just so you can pawn it and eat good for a couple days."

Paige sniffed and wiped away the tear rolling down her cheek. She didn't know anything about her brother, and there was nothing she could do to save him.

Tell him about Me.

"I'm not made of this material, Paige. Do you think I want to steal? No, I don't. Sometimes, I even feel Granny looking down on me. But it's the only way I can get what I need."

"No, it's not," Paige whispered.

"What do you mean, 'no it's not'?"

"No, it's not. It's not the only way. Jesus can help you, Sonny. You know that. Your grandmother raised you to know..."

"Yeah...she did. She dragged me to church every Sunday and then died of a stroke. When she was..."

"It's not about that, Sonny. A relationship with Jesus is not about having a problem-free life. It's about having Someone with you and having peace. Don't you want that?"

"Don't I want what?"

"Peace!" Paige threw her hands up into the air for emphasis.

"Like I said, I been on my own for a long time, and I don't see that changin' by sittin' on a church pew."

"Okay, Sonny. I don't know what else to say."

"There's nothin' else to say. But thanks for bailin' me out, sis." He wrapped his arm around Paige's head and forced her face into his armpit.

"Let go of me, boy," Paige let out a chuckle and tried to push him back. But he held her close. "All right," she said again. "That's enough."

He swatted her bun and smiled, "Aren't you late for class?"

Paige's eyes widened, and she looked at her watch. Ten minutes until class. She was late again.

CHAPTER THIRTY-FOUR

For the next two years, Leslie, Sonny, and Sonya had their ups and downs. Leslie started taking classes at the community college once she got her GED, and said Sonny needed to find a way to contribute to the house.

Sonny, in the meantime, slipped in and out of survival mode, and it landed him in a courtroom again. It wasn't like TV—with lots of people. Here, there was only the courtroom staff, judge, and jury. Sonny tried to smile as he looked out into the courtroom. *Yeah,* he thought, *just like the rest of my life. Nobody here for me. Just like it's always been.*

Paige didn't even show up this time. But she hadn't made an appearance to the last three hearings.

The courtroom kind of reminded Sonny of the church his grandmother used to take him to. The long wooden benches...the jury sitting all together in what could have been a choir loft...the judge wearing a robe like the preacher, except at the end of this day, he wouldn't be asking people to "turn to Jesus." Instead, he'd be handing down a sentence that would determine the next 10 to15 years of his life.

* * *

The county jail smelled of urine and sweat, and the jingle of the warden's keys could be heard loud and clear as he walked down the cell block.

When the keys stopped their clanging, Sonny lifted his head, afraid to hope. But there the warden was, standing at Sonny's cell and giving him the nod. Folks in the jail knew that the warden said as little as possible. Thirty some-odd years of chewing tobacco had caught up with him, and what was left of his teeth and gums was living proof.

The keys started to jingle again, and the warden unlocked the cell.

"Time for my phone call?" Sonny asked as his head popped up from the top bunk. Then he flipped off in one smooth motion and thrust his wrists together between the bars to be cuffed. He had been in jail for two days but decided to wait to place his phone call until he could figure out who was running things and what they wanted.

His looks were his worst enemy here, and he found out it would take two grams of crack to keep from being someone's girlfriend. It all boiled down to Leslie.

As he thought of her, he stuck out his chest and lengthened his stride. He could get Leslie to do anything. It just took a combination of looking into her eyes, wrapping his arm around her waist, and she was his.

The thing is, he hadn't talked to her in a few months, and he wasn't sure, at this point, if his spell had worn off. But come push or shove, Leslie was a ride or die. It just bothered him to be at her mercy.

* * *

"Collect call from…Sonny Jackson…do you accept the charges?" the operator said. Leslie hadn't heard from him in months. *Why is he calling me now?*

"Yes, I'll accept," Leslie said with an eye-roll. *Just like a Negro to call me collect.* She put Sonya in her playpen and lay down on the sofa. Then positioned the phone on her face, so she wouldn't have to hold it with her hands. *This is gonna be good.*

"Leslie?" Sonny cleared his throat two times. "Are you there?"

"Yes. I'm here," Leslie let the chill in her voice tell him just how "happy" she was to hear from him. *Who does he think he is anyway, calling me collect after being ghost for so many months?*

"Uhh…how you been, baby?"

"Don't you baby me, Negro!" Leslie said as she snapped up from her reclined position. She pressed the cordless phone against her ear and mouth to make sure that Sonny could hear every syllable. "The nerve. To call me collect after you ain't said 'boo' to me in three months. I don't know what you think this is, but I am not some side trick you can pick up and put down when you want to. Don't even come at me like that, Sonny Jackson. You hear me?"

Leslie knew Sonny was trying to come up with something sweet to say, and she began to pace the floor back and forth, readying herself with another response. Sonya stood up in her playpen and watched her mother as she paced.

Sonny let out a long breath and repositioned the phone against his ear. No words came to mind that wouldn't set Leslie off.

"You're right, Leslie. You're right. The thing is, I'm in trouble, and you are the only person I can turn to."

"I wish I could say the same for you. I've been taking care of your daughter all by myself, and you float in and out of her life whenever you feel like it. Well, I wish I had someone I could turn to. But I don't, do I, Sonny? Well, I'm not goin' for it anymore. I went to…"

"…college. I know. I know," Sonny tilted his head back and looked toward the ceiling. She always made everything about her. "You went to college, and you don't deserve to be with a loser like me. Listen, Leslie, we've been through all that. Right now, I need a favor…"

Click. And then a dial tone.

"Hello? Hello?" he clicked the receiver to see if the lines had gotten switched. His heart sank into his stomach as he realized Leslie had hung up on him. *How can she do this? I need her right now.*

He used both handcuffed hands to hang up the phone and slowly turned back toward the warden. The warden gave him a knowing smile and used his club to nudge Sonny back toward his cell.

* * *

Leslie sat in silence and tried to force away the tears that came up. She told herself to be strong. But Sonny always had that same effect on her. When he was around, Sonny was good to her. He didn't hit her, steal, or cheat. He just, occasionally, up and left. And her heart melted every time she came home, and he was gone.

More than anything else in the world, Leslie wanted to please Sonny and didn't want to lose him. So she called his cousin to find out what Sonny wanted from her. Then his cousin called a few folks, and within a couple hours, she was headed to the jail with what Sonny needed, tucked safely away in God's pocket book.

CHAPTER THIRTY-FIVE

D eacon Michael Grimes had been coming to the Davidson County Jail every Sunday morning for the past 12 years. Pastor Andrews had brought him along to visit one of the kids from the neighborhood that first Sunday, and before he knew it, he was the head of the Prison and Jail Ministry.

He rarely missed a Sunday after that, and although the names and faces of the inmates changed over the years, their stories were pretty much the same. A young boy, no father to speak of, the wrong friends, and trouble would always seem to find them. Behind these walls and in the small room where Deacon Michael was permitted to hold Bible studies, they all wanted to know that someone cared, that someone would listen, and that they were...worthy.

Sometimes they didn't even get to the lesson, because the young men just wanted to talk. That was okay with Deacon Grimes—he was there to show the love of God. Sometimes that meant setting his sermon aside and listening.

This particular Sunday, the deacon recognized a face he hadn't seen in almost eight years, but he spoke as if he had just met him on the street or in a park.

"Sonny? Sonny Jackson?" he said. "I haven't seen you in a month of Sundays."

"Hey, Coach Grimes," Sonny looked down without making eye contact. The deacon would always be "Coach" to Sonny, even if he was on "deacon business." His orange jumpsuit seemed even itchier, and he fiddled with his sleeve as Coach reached over to hug him. He didn't know what else to say, and the only thought that came to mind was of his granny as he stood there in front of her closest friend. He knew she'd be disappointed.

"How ya doin'?" the coach's hand hadn't left Sonny's shoulder since he hugged him, and his gaze felt like it could stop time.

"Good," Sonny forced his voice to sound more upbeat than he felt. "Just waitin' 'til my time's up."

"Hmm, doesn't look like you're fine. Son, you aren't the same boy I remember running down the basketball court eight years ago. Something's not right."

"I mean, I do miss Granny. Actually, nothin's been right since she left."

"I know what you mean, son. Sorry, I didn't make the funeral. Had a mild stroke the week before and didn't find out she'd passed until I got out of the hospital."

Both men stood in the silence.

"She was an amazing woman, and I hate that I never could get her to be mine," Coach Grimes let a smile spread across his face as he thought about Constance.

Sonny's head jerked up, and the words slipped out before he could catch them. "You had something for my granny?"

Coach Grimes continued to smile as he pulled a couple of chairs closer. "I wouldn't call it just 'something,' Sonny. I loved your grandmother from the first day I saw her at a revival in Stafford, Texas." He leaned back in his chair and began to tell the story.

"We'd both come from small towns in Texas. Wharton was just a few towns over from my hometown. Remember when I drove you, your sister, and Connie there one summer? I always knew your grandmother was going to be something, from the way she held her head and looked straight into people's eyes. White or black." Coach Grimes talked quietly as he revisited the years at Fisk University and all the time he'd spent in the library with Constance, studying Algebra and trying to pass Dr. Sykes' class.

"The thing is, your grandfather, Victor, came along, and turned her head. He was on the football team and a war hero, and I was just a round boy from Stafford. I wanted to build a life with Connie and give her everything she ever dreamed of. But it wasn't in the cards, I guess."

"So you never got married," Sonny said with a sound of finality.

Coach nodded and closed his eyes for a little longer than a blink. He'd been carrying the torch for Constance 45 years, and he'd never given up hope until she passed away.

Sonny felt closer to Coach Grimes than he ever had. Here he was sitting in a jail cell with someone who had loved his granny. And somehow that made her seem closer.

"Now I get why you were always so nice to me," Sonny's eyes smiled as he gently punched Coach Grimes in the shoulder. And Coach rubbed his shoulder pretending to be in pain.

"Okay, enough about that. How are you *really* doin' in here? I know people around here, and I can help you out, if you need it."

Sonny looked into Coach Grimes' eyes, and in them he saw truth. "Ya know, things started out kind-a rough. Some dudes came after me. But I gave them what they wanted, and they haven't bothered me since. So I'm good now."

Coach Grimes frowned and nodded his head. That type of nonsense was a fact of life behind these walls. "Would you like to see Constance again?"

"Yeah."

"Well, you can, if you get to know Jesus."

Sonny let out a sigh and lifted his hand in a dismissive wave. "I'm not trying to get into all that. You know Granny did that church stuff all her life, and she ended up dying from a stroke. So, I think I'll pass."

"Sonny, getting to know Jesus and following Him doesn't mean you don't have problems. It means you have an anchor to hold you down when the storms of life rage," Coach Grimes paused, remembering all the struggles that Constance had faced in her own lifetime. Her life had been so hard, and he had wanted to save her. But she belonged to someone else.

"How do you think Constance managed to stay sane with everything that life threw at her? How was she able to love you? It's because her love for you came from something outside of herself...something other than herself. You can have that love too."

Sonny's body tensed, and he cracked his knuckles. His thoughts began to stew as the pain of losing Constance crept back into his heart. He just wanted to put her out of his mind again and go back to feeling numb.

"Time for me to go," Sonny landed a glare directly at Coach. *Why did he have to remind me of Granny? She's been gone years.*

"Okay, Sonny. It was good seeing you," Coach Grimes said with understanding in his voice. His years of prison visits had taught him when it was time to take a step back. But he tried again anyway. "Lemme tell you one more thing—you need to forgive and let go of your anger. I been tellin' you that for a long time now."

He took even one more risk and tapped his index finger on Sonny's chest. Sonny didn't move. "A lot of stuff has gone wrong in your life, and it ain't been easy. But no mortal man can undo time. And not one of us can change the past. So, son," he moved his hand to Sonny's shoulder and peered into his eyes clouded with visions of all the wrongs that had been done to him, "when the timer's up, I want you to be able to look in your heart and know that you did right. Not by your own standards, but by God inside of you. He's your Father and your Comforter...He won't fail you."

Coach Grimes then pulled out a little green Gideon's New Testament that he carried in his pocket and offered it to Sonny. It was no larger than the size of an index card and was one of the few items he was allowed to give to inmates.

"Nah, I said I'm good," Sonny waved off the Bible and motioned for the guard.

When the guard opened the door for Sonny to walk through, he shot a sympathetic look toward Deacon Grimes. He admired the deacon's persistence, coming here week in and week out, to talk with these hopeless souls. More often than not, the aging man was left holding his little green Bible and sitting alone in silence.

CHAPTER THIRTY-SIX

The lines between night and day blurred for Sonny while he was locked up. He fell into a routine and tried to hold onto the hope that Leslie would come and visit him again soon. But that day never came.

Every time he heard the jingle of the warden's keys coming down the dark corridor toward him, the pace of his heart quickened. Two years had passed since he had made that call to Leslie, and almost every day, he still hoped that she would come back.

Today was a new day, though. When Sonny heard the sound of those keys this time, his head peered off the side of his bunk and into the concrete hallway where the warden stood outside the bars. "You're outta here, Jackson," the warden turned the key to unlock the cell door.

He almost couldn't believe it. Finally, he'd escaped the constant smell of urine and ammonia. He squinted as he exited the building. The sunlight hurt his eyes, and Sonny's heart beat a little faster when he realized that that same light wouldn't be rationed to just two hours a day. He stretched out his arms, closed his eyes, and took a deep breath, allowing the freedom to fill up his lungs.

Leslie's best friend, Rita, waited for him just outside the exit. He wondered why. He hated the way Rita's breath smelled, but he was glad someone was there to meet him.

"Sonny, you got big," Rita eyed him up and down. She had always taken careful note of his build, and the two years of prison workouts had been good to him. He looked a little less brown, and his hair hung down past his ears. He knew better than to get a prison haircut. Only suckers went voluntarily near people with sharp things in jail.

"Yeah. I didn't do much else in there but eat, sleep, and work out," Sonny said, still wondering why Rita was picking him up instead of Leslie. "Where's Leslie?" he finally asked.

"Sonny...be for real. You know good-and-well she's locked up," Rita frowned while unlocking her car door.

Sonny stopped dead in his tracks. He tilted his head sideways and asked "Leslie is in jail? For what?"

"Because of you, Negro. Remember that favor you asked for? Well, they caught her on the way out of the jail. She just got done serving her second year," Rita looked at Sonny with some surprise that he hadn't known. Then she started the engine and pulled the car out of the parking lot.

Sonny rubbed his forehead with his index finger as he buckled his seatbelt. *Where am I gonna stay?* was the first question on his mind. He had planned to stay with Leslie until something else came up. Then he wondered, *What's happened to Sonya since I've been locked up?* But he decided he couldn't worry about that now. He'd have to take first things first.

In about 40 minutes, Rita and Sonny had made the 50-mile trip back to Nashville. The car ride was quiet as Sonny tried to figure out his next move. At some point, Rita offered to let him stay with her until he figured things out.

Deep down, he knew Rita liked him, and he knew that she was Leslie's best friend. But he had nowhere else to go, and going to the mission after just leaving prison was not an option.

* * *

Sonny bounded up the steps to Rita's house and put his one bag of belongings in the corner of the dirty living room floor. He'd already seen several roaches in the less than 30 seconds he'd been in the house and made a mental note to keep his stay short and sweet. For now, he sat straight up on the loveseat, trying not to touch anything.

It wasn't more than a few minutes before Rita sauntered over to him, letting her side rub against him as she sat down. *Finally,* she thought, *I have Sonny Jackson all to myself.* She didn't want Leslie to be in jail, but on the other hand, she had been trying to get close to Sonny since the eighth grade. She liked the way he smelled, the slant of his eyes, and his dark thick curls. And the way he switched back and forth, between his street talk and proper English, depending on who he was with, made her skin tingle.

Now, she would get her chance to have his baby. It would be a pretty one with brown skin and curls, just like him.

CHAPTER THIRTY-SEVEN

Two years had passed since Sonny had come to live with Rita. He hadn't planned to stay that long, but she had made it so easy. She did anything he asked and asked for nothing in return. He didn't have to clean up (Rita didn't do much of that), he didn't have to cook, and he didn't have to watch her kids.

All Rita wanted from Sonny was to be there, and he could do that. Until today. Rita had given him some news—she was pregnant. She beamed as she told him that he was hooked to her for life. Sonny grew real quiet and said he needed some air.

As he walked to the corner store to pick up a Black & Mild, he stroked his beard. Sonny didn't smoke often, but when he did, it helped him sort through things. It took him 20 minutes to cover the two blocks back to Rita's apartment.

As he walked, he seemed to notice everything. The plastic bag trapped in the branches of the leafless tree on the corner. The fire hydrant with no cap—it hadn't been replaced since the kids from the neighborhood pried it open last summer. If there were a fire, the entire block would burn because he knew there wasn't a working fire hydrant for at least ten blocks.

When Sonny made it back to Rita's place, he sat on the stoop to take in the sounds of the falling darkness. The bright orange tip of his unfiltered cigar shone bright as the smell of Chef Boyardee wafted from the kitchen. Rita was no Constance.

His gray jogging pants clung to him in the warm November heat, and he wondered what Carlos would have said about him having two babies by two best friends. Sonny took in a deep inhale and then exhaled the smoke in one smooth blow.

And what would Leslie say? Sonny sat up straight and then let his head hang between his knees. He could almost see her face. The look she would give him. Her eyes would flicker, but then, when he reached out to touch her, they would fill up with moisture. He could always smooth things out with Leslie. He just needed time to explain.

* * *

The guard banged her nightstick on Leslie's cell, and she jumped up out of bed and readied herself for whatever was coming next. It seemed that no matter how hard she tried, she never could sleep the entire night. There was always some noise, some ruckus, and she always woke up in a panic.

"Martinez, letter," the guard shoved the small white envelope through the black rusted bars and gave her an evil smile. "Thought you might like to have this sooner rather than later."

"Thanks," Leslie's heart sped up as she slid the letter out of the envelope, which had already been opened. Something had to be wrong if they were bringing her a letter in the middle of the night. She recognized the smell of her mom's Red Door perfume and realized she really missed her. Despite not having much schooling, her mother had beautiful handwriting as if she were singing onto the page.

Leslie sat on the edge of the bottom bunk and brushed back the loose hair that had escaped from her ponytail. As she held the envelope, her thoughts started to race. *Is something wrong with Mom? Dad? Sonya? Something must be really wrong.* She glanced out into the hallway and saw the guard peering down to the bottom floor. She had her back turned to Leslie and chewed her gum loud enough to wake the dead. *Why is she still hanging around?*

Leslie unfolded the tri-folded letter and focused. It was shorter than she had expected, only a couple of paragraphs. And she began to read.

Mija,

You ain't gonna believe what I found out today. Rita—that slut that claims to be your best friend—is having a baby. By who? Good question. Sonny.

Sonny, the whole reason you're in there. Sonny, the no-good father of your daughter. Sonny, that boy I told you was no good from the beginning.

Thought you'd wanna know.

Te Amo Mucho

Leslie felt her ears pounding, and the page became blurry. *How could he do this?* She had given him everything. Everything. And he still took more.

Adrenaline pulsed through her body, and her eyes darted around the cell looking for something to throw. Ripping the blanket off the bottom bed, she beat her fists against the mattress.

She'd taken him back over and over again. She always took him back. No matter what, because he didn't have anyone else. He needed her. Her. Not anyone else. She gripped the metal frame and buried her face against the bare mattress.

"Why, Sonny? Why?" she wailed. "I did everything you ever asked."

The guard moved toward her cell and grinned. She tapped the bars with her night stick, "That's enough now. Other folks are trying to sleep."

Leslie snarled at her.

"Get some sleep, Martinez. You'll have plenty of time to plot your revenge tomorrow," she winked at Leslie and slipped her nightstick back into her belt-clip.

CHAPTER THIRTY-EIGHT

Four months had passed, and Rita had started to show. Sonny still spent most of his evenings on the porch smoking, because no one had taught Rita that cleanliness was next to godliness. Which also meant that he still kept his belongings in a plastic bin and tried to keep the roaches off his stuff as he plotted his next move.

Tonight, it was raining lightly. But he didn't mind, because it made the street seem closer to clean. He heard footsteps coming up the path, and the face registered. It was Leslie.

Sonny put his Black & Mild on the edge of the stoop and got up slowly.

He ran his hands through his hair and tried to find the words that would fix everything. But no words came. So he decided to walk toward her. She looked small inside the raincoat and matching boots, and from the look on her face, there was no explaining left to do.

Leslie knew everything. As she moved toward Sonny, she buried her hands in her pockets. She was in no hurry. She'd waited, and this was her time. Locking onto his eyes, she tried to make him feel every moment that she'd spent in that cell away from her baby. She tried to make him see how hard she'd worked to get that job with the state. Nothing. Sonny was only sorry that he had gotten caught. Nothing else mattered to him.

Sonny reached out to place both hands on Leslie's shoulders, and his eyes asked for forgiveness—one last time. But this time, it didn't matter. She planted her feet wide, gripped the smooth wooden handle of the knife in her pocket, and lunged for his chest. *How dare you ask for anything when you've already taken everything.*

He tried to hold her arms, but somewhere, somehow, she had help.

Leslie brought the knife up, and down, and in, and out. This was for every time Sonny had left her and the emptiness that had always followed. This was for every late night she had worked to buy food and diapers for Sonya without his help. This was for her heart that longed to stop aching for him, and for the hope he had always killed.

You weren't enough, he heard a voice say.

Sonny grabbed her leg as he slumped to the ground. He looked up at her and mouthed the same words…"I wasn't enough." He knew that he deserved every bit of the rage she'd dished out. Leslie had been nothing but loyal, and he had let her down at every turn. He gasped for air, and his eyelids quivered as he let go of her leg.

Seeing the blood begin to cover his white t-shirt, Leslie dropped the knife and covered her mouth. Then she noticed the blood on her boots and the little black bird that had followed her, sitting not too far off in the shadows.

No…no…no," she whispered. "What did I do?" Leslie stared at her palms as if they had the answer and then slid to the ground. She gathered Sonny's head in her lap. "Sonny. Baby. Please don't leave me. Please."

But he was gone. For good this time.

"Just come back to me. Okay, I'm sorry. Baby. Please," she sobbed. But only the silence answered. As she rocked what was left of him in her arms, she began to scream, "Help us! Somebody, please help us!" She looked back down at his chiseled face.

When Rita heard the screaming, she stepped out onto the porch in her bright pink slippers, and that's when she saw Leslie hunched over Sonny lying on the pavement.

Why is she here? Why is Sonny on the ground? Oh no, oh no…Leslie must know. She saw the blood on the sidewalk where the kids usually played double-dutch and the knife laying near Leslie's lap. As she waddled across the yard, she tried to make sense of the smells, Sonny's face, and Leslie's tears. But nothing registered until she locked eyes with her best friend.

"I don't know what happened," Leslie wiped her nose with the back of her hand. She was still rocking Sonny's head on her lap. "I don't know what happened, Ri. It's like I was in a fog. Then I saw him and just snapped." Leslie forced herself to breathe as the tears rolled down her cheeks. She patted Sonny's face one more time. "What's gonna happen to me, Ri? What's going to happen to my baby?" her voice cracked as the wailing sound of the police siren neared.

* * *

While the flash of blue lights flickered off the building in front of her, Rita grasped for that picture of Sonny on the day she had picked him up from prison. He had looked so good, and she had finally gotten him. But now he was gone again. Rita moved Sonny's head to the sidewalk, took Leslie's hands in hers, and rubbed her cheek. "It'll be okay, girl. I'm here with you."

CHAPTER THIRTY-NINE

As Sonny's breath escaped his body, the pain from his wounds stopped, and he felt a surge of warmth wrap around him. He felt like he was floating, and his cheeks felt flushed.

From his perch above, he watched as Rita tried to calm Leslie. They clung to each other while the ambulance packed up his body and the police marked the crime scene. Even though Leslie was now in handcuffs, the two women were holding each other and rocking as if their entire worlds were being rolled away with the stretcher.

But Sonny felt this strange sense of calm as he watched his body being rolled away. Something felt familiar. Like he'd been here before. And there was a sense of comfort that circled him.

Don't get too comfortable. It won't last, he heard a voice say.

A gentle fog settled around him, and it was difficult to make out Rita and Leslie's faces in the fading light. Seconds later, he couldn't hear their voices anymore, and the stillness came.

Soon, everything seemed to be brighter...lighter...and more translucent. Sonny tried to process what was happening to him as he looked down at a smaller, lighter version of himself suspended in midair next to him. Floating into what seemed like forever, Sonny's feet landed on a hard, cool surface that almost felt like sand, yet it didn't move. The air was thick, and he felt that sense of warmth touch him again. His thoughts froze as he tried to digest his surroundings.

The sun-filled room had no windows, and images of his childhood hung all around at the edges. As he tried to figure out what was happening to him, he concentrated on each picture, one by one, but he couldn't recall some of the moments.

He did recognize the life-sized photo of his third birthday party. It was the same picture that his granny had given him when he turned 13. Sonny reached out to touch his dad's one-dimensional face and stared into his eyes.

Just then, a large hand squeezed Sonny's shoulder, and he shot a glance at a man standing behind him. The man's face looked familiar, yet Sonny had to fight off the urge to take off running. It seemed as if he had met this man before, and he grasped at the corner of his mind trying to remember.

"Sonny, come with Me. There are some things I want to explain to you before you go to rest." Stillness settled over Sonny as the man spoke. His voice was comforting yet heavy, and they shared the same tawny orange-brown color. He was tall, and as He walked toward the end of the room, Sonny followed before he had the chance to make up his mind.

"Excuse me, but, do I know You?" he cleared his throat and tried to control the sensations that kept running through him.

"Yes and no. Yes, we've met before. But, no, you don't know Me, at least not in the way I had planned. But I'll explain all of that later. We don't have much time. Your body just died, and it won't be long before your soul," the Father motioned toward the translucent version of Sonny that was floating in front of Him, "has to leave."

He then turned around and picked up His pace.

Before Sonny could respond, colors swirled around him, and he felt as if he were in the middle of a tornado. But he wasn't afraid this time. Growing up, the sound of thunder had always scared him, and he would climb into bed with Constance whenever there was a storm. She would always say, "No need to be afraid. It's just the Good Lord talking." But that logic always failed to comfort him. For some reason, though, today was different.

"By the way," the Father said, "that sense of calm that you're feeling is something that people search their whole life for. They meditate and ohm, but that sense of peace they're searching for comes only when you are with Me. Your spirit came back to Me today, and that's the sense of belonging you are feeling. But your soul...well, I'll explain all of that in the time we have left together."

Sonny wasn't listening, though. He was too focused on the screen that had popped up in front of him.

* * *

"Wait. Where am I?" Sonny asked as his mind raced. He tried to stand still, but for some reason, he kept following the man.

"Well," the Father said, turning to look at Sonny and letting His warm gaze fall around him, "you are in the eternal...some call it Heaven. I just call it home." The Father smiled and stood still to see if Sonny had any more questions.

"Uh –huh," Sonny said with a half-nod. He had more questions than answers, and he shifted from one foot to the other. He noticed that the man was waiting for him to say something else, so he forced out "I-I guess I'm ready to go on now."

Something was strange about this man, but he couldn't put his finger on it.

The Father, sensing he was uneasy, asked, "Would you like to see some of your happy times?"

At first, Sonny's face lit up, and then frowned with a look of confusion. He could barely remember having any happy times. But he followed the man into the room.

The ceilings were so high he couldn't see them, and a large screen the size of a football field had popped up to his left. Everything looked strange, yet for some reason, he felt at ease. And Sonny couldn't shake the feeling that he'd been here before.

The Father motioned towards an empty space in front of the screen and asked Sonny to have a seat. A chair appeared, and before Sonny could make a decision to comply, he was sitting in front of the screen.

"Do you remember when you and your mother went to the ocean when you were six years old?" the Father began. "Aside from the night she came to your senior basketball game, it was your only happy memory with her."

Up popped an image of him, Rachel, and Paige walking on the beach. Rachel was holding his hand, and her hair blew in the wind as she looked down to smile at him. Sonny had forgotten about the trip to Panama City. It seemed like such a long time ago.

"You liked the beach and splashing in the waves," the Father continued, "and you loved the water. It was the only vacation that you ever took with your mom and sister, and you hated that you had to leave Rachel." He looked at Sonny and smiled.

Sonny made eye contact and grinned sheepishly. He had acted a fool when his mom told him it was time to go back home.

"How do You know all this about me?"

"I know everything about you. I have always known your every thought, your every fear, your every hope." He took a seat beside Sonny, placed His hand on his knee, and continued. "I'm your Father. That's how I know everything about you."

Sonny caught his breath when he heard the word "father." *What does this man mean? My dad died a long time ago.*

Reading his thoughts, He continued, "Even though your dad, Victor Junior, wasn't around to provide for you, protect you, and show you your identity, I've always been there. I made the world, like my home here, because I wanted you to always have that sense of peace and calm you had that day at the beach with your mother and sister."

"Wait. What?" Sonny's voice cracked. "What do you mean You were always there to protect me? Do You even know about my life? No one was there. All I ever had was me," Sonny clenched his fist and narrowed his eyes.

"Yes, I was there. I was there every moment, and I'm just about to prove it to you."

Up on the screen flashed a bright light—the brightest light Sonny had ever seen, and he grew quiet. That strange familiar feeling was creeping up again. He knew this light, but, he couldn't remember where he knew it from.

"This is the star that I hung in the sky when you were born. It is your star. I hang a new one every time a new soul is born, and every soul is assigned a guardian angel. Scientists say that the universe is continuing to expand—no great insight, mind you—but it is expanding in the sense that every time a soul is born, an angel takes up residence in the sky as a star. The stars show evidence of the connection between heaven and earth."

Sonny sat down on the floor Indian-style and ran his hands through his hair. *What's happening here?* he wondered. *What does all this mean?*

The Father chimed in again, "I was going to save this for later, but let Me explain it now. I've always been with you." He sat down on the floor next to Sonny and began to draw a picture on the sandy surface.

"Your spirit—the small version of you that you saw earlier when the ambulance took your body—is a piece of Me. I gave it to you before you were born. Before Rachel carried you in her belly, I knew you. This larger version of you—the one sitting here with Me now—is your soul. Your soul was what you chose to follow while you lived your life."

"Wait. I don't feel like I was given a choice. No one ever explained all this to me," Sonny said as he took his head out of his hands to look deeper into the Father's eyes.

Time stopped.

And He felt a tingle.

"You were given a chance, Sonny. Numerous chances. I'll show you a few later, but for right now, let Me finish explaining your soul."

The Father paused, and when Sonny nodded, He continued.

"All souls have the power to choose. Had you chosen to follow Me, you could have accessed My power and the assistance of your angel to help you finish your mission on earth. But your soul did not follow your spirit, because you never knew Me."

"What was my mission?"

The Father smiled and placed his hand on Sonny's shoulder. "Oh, son, the mission I had for you was to solve one of the earth's most pressing problems. Remember that whenever you spoke, people always listened to you and did whatever you said? That was one of the gifts I gave you for your mission. I can't tell you the mission, however, because it has been reassigned to someone else."

"Reassigned?" Coldness filled Sonny's core.

"Yes. I have a purpose for every soul. But if a soul chooses not to follow My voice, the mission is reassigned once that soul leaves the earth. And the mission continues to be reassigned until someone carries it out. Now your grandmother, Constance," a smile spread across His face, "she did well. She was faithful to her mission. She's now with Me here forever."

"Granny is here?" Sonny stood up and imagined what it'd be like to see her. "Where is she?" he began to pace back and forth.

"No, Sonny. You won't get to see her. She is out of reach to you because of the decisions you made. But I am going to let you see your grandfather. Seeing him will explain a lot of your own story."

CHAPTER FORTY

The Father wrapped his arms around Sonny's shoulders and covered his face. They were moving at the speed of light, and all Sonny could feel was the wind swirling at his back. It was cold, and his hair stood up on end, but he felt warm and relaxed at the same time. Eventually, they arrived at what appeared to be a dirt road.

"I'm going to show you a glimpse of your grandfather's childhood—when he was just a little boy. It will help you better understand him," the Father explained.

Sonny peered into the screen and saw what looked like a farm. Chickens were running around in front of a broken-down house, and a sparse wooden fence lined the property.

* * *

The August heat had settled in for the afternoon on the Humphrey farm. The family had worked shares for years to purchase this farm, and owning their own land made them pillars of the community.

It hadn't rained for more than three weeks, and the dust had settled on everything from the kitchen counter to the faces of the children who had come down for the summer to pick cotton. Victor was charged with feeding the hogs. So he took a break from the field around 2:00 every day. But today, something felt different.

He headed to the back of the house to grab the scraps from breakfast and add them to the mush to feed the animals. He held the mush bucket with one hand and his nose with the other. He hated this part of the day. The pigs in all their slop made him wish that the summer was over and he was back in school. As quickly as he could, he threw the slop in the bin and headed to the wash tub to bathe.

He slipped out of his clothes and into the cold water. It had been used a few times, but it was better than the feeling of slime that stuck to him after being near the hogs. As he continued to wash up, he heard a rustle in the corner of the barn.

Uncle Willie. He hated being alone in a room with him.

"Hey, Uncle Willie, what are you doin' here?" Victor said as he sunk low in the tub and tried to submerge as much of his body as possible.

"Came to see you, boy. Knewed you be in here," Willie replied as he unbuckled his overall strap and lumbered over toward him. He licked his lips; and in one motion his overalls were off, and he was standing there naked except for his boots.

"Wh-what are ya doin'? You don't take a wash at this time." Victor's stomach felt sick. Deep down, he knew why Uncle Willie was there. There had been whispers and warnings to stay away from him.

But on this hot day in August, he had nowhere to go and no one to protect him.

* * *

"Sonny, do you remember when the same thing happened to you while at the county jail?"

Sonny looked down at this feet. His spine ached as he remembered the day he went to take a shower and three men came in after him. There had been no one there to protect him. He had felt so alone.

The next day, Leslie delivered what he'd asked for, and the men never came for him again.

"Would you take a walk with Me?" the Father said.

"Do I got a choice?"

"You always have a choice," the Father replied as He turned and placed His hand on his shoulder and peered into his eyes. Sonny looked away. The Father's eyes were too piercing, and right now, under His gaze, he just wanted to run. But there was nowhere to go.

"Yeah. I'll come."

The Father led Sonny back to the beach where his mother had taken him and Paige. "Remember the time Constance gave you that chain from your grandfather and the picture of your family on your third birthday?"

"Yeah, it was just before she died."

"Well, she mentioned something about African traditions, and at the time, you didn't really understand what she meant. So I want to explain them to you before we go to your next piece of history."

"I'm not really interested in this," Sonny interrupted. "I'm just ready to get outta here and understand what's goin' on with me."

"You will, Sonny. The time will come, and you'll wish for the time you were back here. But explaining this will help you understand some things about your life."

The Father sat down on the edge of the pier and motioned for Sonny to have a seat beside him. Reluctantly, Sonny sat down an awkward three feet away. He was tired of being around this man he knew nothing about, but who seemed to know every detail about him.

He just wanted to get on with whatever was coming and leave this sense of nothingness alone. The pain felt more familiar.

"Constance was trying to explain to you the duty to your community, Sonny. When she gave you that chain and the picture of your mom and dad, she was trying to tell you that you are greater than all the stuff that's happened to you. She wanted you to know that you are connected to the past and to the future and that there are lots of people who have loved you."

"Do you even know what I was up against? I never had a chance," Sonny got up to walk away but remembered he didn't even know where to go.

"Don't walk away from Me. You've done that one too many times already," the Father's voice changed, and the force was noticeable.

Sonny turned around to face Him, before the Father continued. "You did have a shot. Everyone does. You had a purpose, and your soul came out of the spirit world to fulfill that purpose. I made you because your community needed your gifts and talents to solve a traumatic problem."

"Well, why didn't You just tell me that?"

"It doesn't work like that. It is the responsibility of the elders to help you understand your purpose and mission in life. You were surrounded by elders like Coach Grimes and Constance, but you decided early on that you weren't going to listen to them. You wanted to do your own thing. And you were left to fend for yourself."

"But they were whack! Coach and Granny was always tryin' to control me."

"Sonny, I put them in your life to help guide you from one stage of life to another. You were looking for a guide," the Father tapped him on the chest with his index finger. "Everyone is looking for a guide. You just picked the wrong one."

Silence filled the air as the Father sent memories of Carlos back to him. Sonny wanted to belong. He'd gotten tired of being alone, and Carlos came along and filled that void. It was just a convenient bonus that Carlos was big enough to be a linebacker and gave him a little protection.

Coach wasn't there when he had to walk home in the dark after practice and cross the street, back and forth four times, just to keep from running into the wrong people. Every move meant something. A nod. No nod. Eye contact. No eye contact. The wrong nod or the wrong eye contact could mean a beat-down or worse. Granny didn't know what it all meant, and she didn't understand the thin line of survival he walked every day. *Carlos did.* Carlos did, and Carlos made that line just a little bit wider.

"Carlos protected me, though. When no one else was there, he was there for me."

"Carlos did help you *once*. But he got you into far more trouble than he ever got you out of. You remember that time at Mr. Young's?"

Sonny let out a sly grin as he looked out into the distance. He did remember that day. It seemed like it had just happened, but more than 12 years had passed.

"At that time, you were on the brink of becoming a man. Trying to be a man. You were searching, and Carlos came around just in time to lead you astray."

"Wait. What do you mean he led me astray?"

"Look at all the bad things you got into when Carlos came around. Stealing, lying, skipping school, and fighting. You didn't do any of that until you started running with him."

The memories of Carlos continued to flash before him, but this time, they were mixed with *before* Carlos and then the memories *after* Carlos. Before Carlos—perfect attendance, making birthday dinners for Constance, honor roll, and helping Coach Grimes fix up his old Chevy. After Carlos—nights out after the street lights came on, Sunday mornings pretending to be sick so he could skip church, lots of days in detention, and a few days of suspension. *Okay, okay, Sonny thought, I got into some trouble with Carlos. But Carlos was family, and he kept me safe.*

"Look, I didn't bring you here to talk about Carlos. I came to talk about the path that you were supposed to be on. May we continue?"

"Yeah," Sonny said. The man had a point—things had taken a turn when he and Carlos had started hanging out together.

"You don't all of sudden become an adult when you hit a certain age. That's why I put elders into your life to help guide you. But, you chose not to listen to them or to let them in. So you always felt alone and just drifted without an anchor. Yet those people had been placed there to help teach you the skills you needed for life, help you put away childish things, and help you find your identity. Most importantly, they were there to help you live a life without fear and to find peace."

CHAPTER FORTY-ONE

Another swirl, and Sonny was at another farm, one that was larger and with green rolling hills stretched as far as he could see. Rows and rows of white fluffy bolls filled the field, and men, women, and children hunched over those bolls and picked as fast as they could.

A man sat on his horse in the distance and occasionally cracked his whip over the back of one of the slower-moving pickers. The heat of the day was bearing down on them, and the sweat glistened off their chocolate-colored bodies as each one tried to pick faster than the one beside him. Picking faster helped avoid the lashes.

"Sonny," the Father placed his hands on his shoulder and peered into his eyes, "our next stop is going to be extremely difficult for you. But I need you to see what happened to your great-great-grandfather. It will help you make sense of everything."

Sonny nodded solemnly and took a deep breath. Something felt heavy, and he was not looking forward to whatever came next. Still, a feeling of comfort settled over him as the Father took his hand.

* * *

Sonny blinked, and they were in a dark log cabin that smelled of dried meat and animal fat. He wrinkled his nose as the smell filled his nostrils. When his eyes adjusted to the darkness, he could make out the figures of three women chained to the walls where the sides of meat and beef also hung.

The women were whimpering yet trying not to show the fear that was gripping their hearts. Each one had strong shoulders and muscles that protruded from her back. They were the fastest pickers of cotton, rarely got sick, and bore strong children that got a good price at the auction. For their reward, they were selected to continue increasing the master's property holdings.

Once a year, the strongest of the male slaves in the county was rented out to neighbors who could afford to breed. This year, Frank had been selected for the duties along with the three strongest women on the Jackson plantation.

The owners and their overseers peered through the cracks in the shed and took bets on the ability of the selected stud to perform his duties in record time.

"Frank was your great-great-grandfather," the Father said in a low solemn tone.

Sonny took a deep breath in and tried to make out his face. Frank looked just like the pictures he'd seen of his grandad—dark skin, large jaws, and drooping shoulders. His eyes also had that hollow look, as if his entire soul had been emptied of any feeling.

Frank was shoved into the shed, and his cheek grazed the dirt floor as he fell to the ground. He used his chained hands to sit himself up and sat staring at his feet to avoid making eye contact with the women. He knew what was to come next, and sorrow gripped his heart as he realized there was no way out.

Everything seemed to happen in slow motion. Frank was unchained, and the defenseless naked women began to whimper louder. Even though they'd endured the annual event many times...it never eased their pain. They had husbands who they were forced to betray, daughters that knew the same thing would happen to them someday, and sons that might become this monster.

The spectators peering through the cracks were enjoying themselves—breeding was good sport. Meanwhile, the overseer collected their bets, and their laughter pierced the background as the event got underway.

Every eye locked onto Frank, and he performed as if he was on auto pilot. One after the other, he planted his seed into the women he'd never laid eyes on before. He tried to finish as quickly as possible, just to get the deed over with.

Then Frank sunk to the floor in exhaustion, sweat dropping from his brow. He decided it was too much to take the third woman, and he'd rather die here than go on.

Whack! Whack!

Two sharp lashes ripped skin from his back. But he ignored the pain. Death would be a sweet end.

Whap! Whap!

But this time, Frank felt no sting. He looked up from the ground to see the overseer taking out his rebellion on the final woman, and it was more than he could bear. It was one thing to be beaten to his own death, but he could not let a woman suffer the whip on his account.

Frank scrapped himself off the ground and continued with the task he'd been brought there to do. He couldn't make eye contact with Sally, the third and last woman. The pain showed on her face and was far worse than the pain that came from the lash ripping across his back.

Finally, he finished. His eyes were vacant, and his mind was numb as he thought about the lives his children would face. Slumping to the ground in defeat, Frank let out an aching sob.

"You did good, boy," the overseer said as he slapped Frank on the shoulder. "Now, let's see what you got left." He dropped his pants, whip in hand, and continued his quest to rip every shred of dignity from Frank's being.

Sonny cowered in the corner and tried to hide his face from the horror that he had just witnessed. He wanted to escape the sounds and the sense of terror that hung in the air. With one look, he begged the Father to get him out of there.

* * *

The Father wrapped Sonny in His presence, and Sonny felt a cool breeze. The pace of his heart gradually steadied as they put the drying shed in the distance.

"How could You let that happen?" Sonny cried as he clenched his fist. "You stood there and did nothing, while all that bad stuff was happening."

"Sonny," the Father said after taking a deep breath, "I give people free will. I cannot override their free will with what I want. What you witnessed there opened the door to the spirit world. And for many generations, children of those slaves have been abandoning their own children."

Sonny shook his head in disbelief. He couldn't believe the Father could sit by like some sucker. And now, He was standing here so close, their chests almost touched.

The Father wrapped His hands around Sonny's shoulder and said, "Sit down. Let Me explain."

Sonny collapsed into the chair. Exhausted from everything he'd just seen, he rubbed his temples and tried to focus on what the Father was saying. His voice faded in and out.

"What happened to you at the jail and to your grandfather in the shed that summer, it all began many years ago. It took root there in that drying shed. Do you understand?"

Sonny *didn't* understand, but he nodded anyway. He didn't understand why he had to go through all that stuff or why his life had to be so hard. All that horrible stuff that had happened so many years ago had nothing to do with him. *And how could this man stand by and do nothing while it all happened?*

"Frank never connected with his children or with their mothers. This type of thing happened hundreds of thousands of times during slavery in the United States as families were ripped apart, and it weakened their sense of community. That is why you could often get up and leave your Leslie and Sonya without a second thought—because family connections and a sense of duty to your community were broken hundreds of years ago during slavery and colonialism."

Sonny sat and remembered the time he moved in with Colleen. He'd left Leslie with Sonya still growing inside her and hadn't even said goodbye. After Colleen kicked him out, Leslie still took him back.

"That curse of fathers abandoning their children was placed on your family generations ago, and you all are still paying the price."

Sonny didn't say anything.

"The best thing a father can do for his children is to love their mother," the Father said. "It is through that lens that those children view Me, their heavenly Father, and can know that they are unconditionally loved and accepted."

Sonny nodded and thought about the two children he'd left behind. He wondered what would happen to them now that their mother was a murderer and he was dead.

"When Frank was emancipated in 1865, his body was set free to do whatever it wanted, but his soul was still enslaved to that curse. Everything he'd known was related to slavery—how he got his food, clothing, and value. As long as he produced slaves, he was considered valuable, but once he was a freed man, there was no one there to give him direction. He was an orphan, and all his decisions were based solely on survival."

Sonny looked into the Father's eyes and tried to make sense of what he was seeing. But he became overwhelmed with the fact that Frank's story was his story. The reason he felt lost was that his great-great-grandfather had felt the same sense of loss when his body was "emancipated." He had felt that same sense of drifting the day of his 18th birthday when he aged out of foster care. He had been given a week's work of clothes, a debit card, and was told to check in and finish high school.

"Frank could not read or write. His family was systemically ripped apart, he had no property, and he had no foundation to build a life upon. He spent the rest of his life wandering in and out of various women's homes, just like you did, and working whenever he felt like it. The years of being held captive had left his soul broken and empty. Afterward, he spent his life searching for provision and protection, and died still trying to prove he was worthy. He was murdered by a husband who found him in bed with his wife. Did you know that?"

Sonny just wanted to be alone. *Another murder in my family? How come all the men in my family died unnatural deaths? Not one of them lived to see gray hair.*

"Yes, all the men in your family were haunted by the same curse, and many of them still tie their value to the amount of children they produce."

"How come Granny never told me about this?"

"She was ashamed of what happened to him, so she just kept it quiet all those years. Your grandmother knew Me though. That's why she was able to remain peaceful despite all the turmoil that you, Victor Junior, and Victor Senior wrought on her life."

"She still died, though."

"Yes, her death was a little premature. But she simply couldn't bear to see you go down the road that Victor Junior took. The stress from the past and what you put her through led to the stroke, son. It didn't matter in the end, though, because she is with Me. She isn't in pain, and she no longer worries."

The Father walked toward the screen again and motioned for Sonny to come along. Sonny let out a sigh and followed even though he didn't feel like it.

"Now, there are some more things I want to show you about your life. Remember earlier, when I said you'd had several brushes with death?"

"Yeah, I remember."

"Well, now I'm going to show you how I protected you all of those years and the chances that I gave you to accept Me, see Me, and know Me. Are you ready to continue our history lesson?"

Sonny shrugged. Then he mentally readied himself for their next stop.

CHAPTER FORTY-TWO

Rachel pulled at the neck of her light gray sweatshirt with "Central Tennessee Mental Health Facility" printed across the left side in faded navy blue letters. The clock read 2:47 p.m. The mail would be circulated in a few minutes, and she waited near the nursing station for the attendant to call out the names.

She leaned on the counter of the nursing station and tried not to look at the clock every few seconds. Looking at the time only prolonged the wait. Waiting. That's all her life consisted of these days. Waiting for a visit, waiting for a letter, waiting for a call...anything to know that someone was thinking of her and wondered how she was doing.

Constance wrote every few months to tell her about Sonny. But she hadn't even heard from her in a while. Maybe today would be different. Maybe she'd hear about her son. Maybe Constance would say that he'd asked about her. Or that he wanted to come and visit.

She hadn't seen him since that day on the sidewalk. He'd spit on her. Her own flesh and blood—her son—had spit on her. Every millisecond of that moment transported her back to the day she told her dad that she was pregnant with him. That day, her dad and everything she believed about him broke into a million pieces. Now, she just wanted a new memory of her son. She *needed* a new memory of her son. Why didn't he call? Why didn't he visit? Didn't he care?

"Octavia Wright," the attendant looked around at the small group gathered around the nursing station and held the yellow envelope up in the air.

An ebony-colored woman with smooth skin and empty eyes moved toward the attendant. Then she shook her head slightly and whispered to the attendant who opened the envelope and tucked it under the lady's arm. She forced a slight smile and shuffled off to the sitting room.

"Richard Jones," the attendant called next.

Rachel stared at the one gray tile on the floor. Every so often, the floor was accented with a pink tile among the gray ones. There were 427 pink tiles and 563 grey tiles in her unit. Once, she had passed three days by counting and recounting to make certain that she didn't miss any of them. She'd tried counting other things, but usually lost track.

"Amy Johnson."

Rachel's birthday was next week. Surely someone would remember her on her birthday. When she was growing up, it was the only time she got to be the center of attention. Her dad would come home from work early, and her parents would take her anywhere she wanted to eat. There was even one time when she was 13 that she broke with tradition and asked them to take her rolling skating. Neither of them could skate, but they took her anyway. Her last birthday party was her sweet 16.

That party had been at the movie theater, and her parents had let her invite boys. That was when Victor Junior had given her the best gift ever—that little silver butterfly necklace. She had put it on her neck that day and had never taken it off until...*someone has to remember my birthday.*

"Kelisa Armstrong."

She wasn't getting any mail today. Today was just like all the other days. *Why do I keep hoping?* "God, just give it up already," she whispered to herself as she wiped away the moisture forming in her eyes. *It doesn't matter anyway. I have everything I need—food, clothing, shelter.*

"That's all for today, folks," the attendant raised the empty mail basket for everyone to see, and the small group dispersed with a quiet grumble. Rachel lifted her head from the crook in her arm and remembered she needed to quit putting herself through this. She needed to stop hoping. All she had was her.

She tried to ignore the pain she felt from the hole in her heart. Sometimes she could numb the feeling, but today was not one of those days. She cleared her throat and approached the attendant. "Excuse me, could I get something for my head," she tapped her temple. "The voices are coming back."

The attendant laid her hand on Rachel's shoulder and looked directly at her. The lady's eyes were soft and kind and reminded Rachel of the way Constance looked at Sonny when he was a baby. The attendant then gave Rachel's shoulder a gentle squeeze. As the warmth traveled through her arm, she closed her eyes to hold back the tears.

"Sure, Miss Andrews. Why don't you go lie down? I'll get your chart and talk to the nurse. We should be back in a few minutes."

Rachel took a deep breath, nodded, and shuffled back to her assigned bed. In a few minutes, everything would be quiet and numb, and that's what she needed most.

Sonny watched as his mother slumped into bed and stared blankly at the ceiling. She seemed to be counting. Or maybe mumbling. She really *was* crazy. All those times he'd been waiting for her to call, she'd been in the crazy house. But she was the adult. She should have gotten herself together.

"Rachel spent her life trying to cope...trying to ease the pain. Her father's abuse, your dad's murder, her mother's harshness—it all led to soul wounds that never healed, and it landed her here," the Father said.

"She should have tried harder. She had three kids that needed her. I *needed* her. Why didn't You do anything?"

"I *did*. Rachel's going to have her chances, just like you did."

"I didn't have a chance. I *never* had a chance. From day one, everything was against me."

"You had it tough—there is no doubt about that. But I saved your life on three separate occasions just so you would have a chance," the Father placed his hand on Sonny's shoulder. "The first time happened before you were even born. I used the necklace your dad got your mom for her birthday."

Sonny vaguely remembered seeing the necklace around Rachel's neck. She used to wear it all the time.

"We are a little off track, though. The whole point of this visit is to help you understand that your mother couldn't give you what she never had. Do you understand?"

"Not really. She should have been there. No excuses."

"Sonny, she couldn't give you what she didn't have. You had Constance, which is more love than your mother ever had."

He took a step back as he heard the Father's voice say what he'd always felt.

"Look at Me," the Father shook his shoulders and pierced him with His gaze. "Listen, you suffered from rejection in the womb. Yes, your mother didn't want you. The enemy always tries to destroy people, hopes, and dreams in their infancy, so they don't take root and grow. But I sent your angel to fight for you."

"What angel?"

"Your messenger that I mentioned earlier when we talked about the stars. He was the one who reminded Rachel to talk to Victor Junior. That memory saved your life."

Sonny sat in silence, and he continued to think about his mother until he remembered the time he'd seen Rachel on the street with that john. That thought of her made his blood boil. After that, he'd done his best to push her out of his memory.

"After your father's death, Rachel succumbed to the darkness of the curse, and she couldn't get out. Every day she woke up, she wanted it to be her last, and that is why she started taking the pills. She was trying to escape, but she didn't want to ask Me for help."

* * *

Sonny sat on the grassy knoll and attempted to still the feelings that wanted to escape. A mix of sadness, loss, and anger welled up in his throat, and he couldn't get rid of them. At this point, he just wanted to get away from the Father. It was just too much to think about right now.

"Two more visits Sonny, and then you can rest."

Sonny scraped himself up off the ground so he could follow the Father into the next time period. He couldn't imagine what would happen next.

CHAPTER FORTY-THREE

A three-year-old version of himself, which looked just like the picture his granny had given him, zipped down the block on a North Caroline blue tricycle. A tall man jogged beside him with his hands on his shoulder.

"Good job, Sonny," Victor Junior called out as he looked down at his son and smiled. "I'm proud of you." Sonny didn't look up, he just kept right on pedaling. His dad bent down to tie his shoe and then threw a rock at the approaching night-colored pigeon.

Two guys walked up behind him and told him to give up his shoes and jacket. He said, "No," and shoved one of the guys to the ground, then jumped on him and began pounding his face.

"You thought 'cause I'm out here with my son, you could just creep up on me like that, huh?" Victor Junior said. "Well, I'm not goin' out like no punk."

The other guy yelled for Victor Junior to stop hitting his brother. He didn't. Victor was going to make them pay. They'd never try to rob another soul.

Bang. Bang. Bang.

Victor Junior slumped to the ground. Blood spread across his UNC starter jacket and gathered in a pool around his body. The two guys ran off as Sonny rounded the block and circled back to see his father laying on the pavement gasping for air.

"Da-da, Da-da," Sonny cried as he steered his tricycle as close as possible and tumbled off of it into a pile.

"Sonny, it's gonna be okay," Victor Junior gasped. "It's gonna be fine. I want you to know that I love you more than anything in the world. I'll always, always be there for you." He gripped his small boy against him and held his gaze as long as he could, until his body went limp.

Sonny patted his face and tried to wake him up. But all his breath was gone.

* * *

The Father cleared His throat to get Sonny's attention. "Does this remind you of anything?"

Sonny sat there quietly and stared at his feet as if he was waiting for an answer to appear in the ground. He hoped this moment was all a dream and he'd wake up in Leslie's arms.

Sonny took a deep gulp and said, "Yes, me and my dad were the same."

"That's right. Even though your deaths were two decades apart, the curse your family lived under was still at work. The guys wanted what your dad had and took his life, just like Leslie wanted you back from Rita."

Sonny shook his head and tried to rationalize the similarities. It wasn't his fault. He didn't know that he had repeated the cycle—that there even was a cycle. No one had told him any of this.

"That was the second attempt on your life. The third one involved you and Carlos. You remember that hole in your hoodie after Carlos was killed?"

Sonny nodded.

"But I wouldn't let you leave the world until you had ample chances to accept Me. You never did, though. So now, you must go and rest."

The finality of the Father's words sank into Sonny's gut. Now he must go to rest. He tried to remember everything he'd seen and how it was all connected. His body had been carted away in the back of the ambulance. His spirit, that smaller version of him, which was a little piece of the Father, would stay here. And the soul—the mind, will, and emotions—of him would go to rest and leave the Father forever.

Now, again, Sonny was being sent away.

CHAPTER FORTY-FOUR

Leslie and Rita sat with Sonny until the ambulance and the police came to remove his body. Rita explained everything to Leslie and told her she was sorry she'd taken him. Rita had betrayed the only person who had ever been kind to her.

Leslie just sat there, though, not saying anything. She had stroked Sonny's colorless face until they had taken him away. She had given Sonny everything she had. And he had always found a way to make her feel that she was not quite good enough. Now, the love of her life was gone. And she could no longer chase his acceptance.

Leslie took a deep breath and nodded when Rita promised to take care of Sonya while she was away. They both knew she'd be away for a long time. Deep down, though, Leslie hoped Sonny's sister, Paige, would step up to the plate and care for her daughter.

As the ambulance crew loaded Sonny into the ambulance, Leslie thought they were being a bit rough with him. *They should be showing more respect. But he's probably just another dead, black man to them, headed to the morgue for a toe tag.*

Leslie allowed the officer to help her up from the ground. She straightened her dress the best way she could with her hands cuffed and gave Rita one last look as the officer led her toward the police car.

Things would go easier if she didn't fight.

That was the problem. She had been fighting her whole life, and this is where it had landed her, with blood on her boots.

CHAPTER FORTY-FIVE

S onny sat back with the Father and listened to the crash of the ocean hitting the rocks. It sounded as though they were now in a long tunnel, where freedom and light would come out on the other end. The air was crisp and clean, and his memory flashed back to Panama City Beach again. It was the best memory he had of his mother, and he wanted to hang onto it.

Sonny and the Father waded into the water until they were waist-deep in the waves. The Father then handed Sonny a baited fishing rod and patted him on the shoulder.

"I don't really know what I'm doing," Sonny said as he held the rod at an awkward angle and tried to figure out how to make it work. "I've only seen fishing on TV."

"Just drag the bait over the top of the water, and the fish will come to you," the Father said as He gently straightened Sonny's arms and demonstrated the correct way to attract the Silver Salmon that occasionally came to the surface.

"Remember Coach Grimes?" He turned to Sonny, and a smile spread across His face as the salmon began to jump and try to catch the bait.

"Yeah. I remember him. He didn't come to Granny's funeral, though."

"He was in the hospital...the stuff you remember and what you choose to forget never cease to amaze Me...he did visit you in jail. You remember that?"

Sonny nodded.

"See, he was one of your elders. Coach Grimes was one of the people I placed in your life to tell you about Me and show you My love. But you always pushed him away. Why was that?"

"Don't know," Sonny shrugged.

"That's why you always felt alone in your life. Not because people left you, but because you never accepted Me. Sure, you got temporary approval from Leslie, Colleen, Rita, and all the other ones. But the peace you were always looking for only comes from Me."

Sonny didn't respond. The Father was right. Each one of those girls had tried to please him, but he always felt empty.

"I've been trying to catch you with moments like that your whole life. It's similar to the way you are trying to catch that salmon."

"What do you mean you've been trying to catch me?"

"Some people call Me a fisherman. I am always trying to draw people closer and bring them to Me. I bait them by placing My children in their lives to show them light, peace, love, and unconditional acceptance. But many times, they are ignored."

"I didn't ignore them! Granny, Paige, and Coach were just trying too hard and doing too much and I couldn't get with that life."

"I'll agree with you there. Many of My children live a life that makes following Me seem like a chore, but there are others who understand the real adventure. People like George Washington Carver and Frederick Douglass. These were great men who lived out the purpose and the adventure I had for them."

Sonny stood still and tried to process what the Father had said.

"Constance, Michael Grimes, Paige, and Mr. Young—all of them are My followers. And your guardian angel protected you from death, just so you could hear the message from them."

The memories rushed back to Sonny, including the time that Paige had met him at the courthouse and tried to explain that he didn't have to be alone. Coach Grimes had tried to explain to him the cure for his anger and pent-up rage. And Granny...he remembered all the times she had prayed for him when she thought he was asleep in bed. He waited for that prayer and the moment she would sneak in quietly with her rocking chair. It always gave him comfort, and many times, he couldn't sleep without it.

The salmon jumped, and Sonny stood up straight, reminding himself that he couldn't swim. There was a lot of water here to swallow, and he was not about to drown after he'd already been stabbed to death in the same day. That was a bit much for even him. "You know that part of you that didn't want to steal from Mr. Young the day you and Carlos took those Oreos?" asked the Father.

Sonny nodded, not wanting to make eye contact again.

"That was Me speaking to your spirit. That was part of Me that is in you. Some people call it their conscience, or the little voice inside their head, or other superstitious sayings. The fact of the matter is, it was Me speaking to you. You heard Me speak to you a lot when you were younger. But as you got older, you heard Me less and less."

Sonny remembered the feeling of guilt that had swept over him as he and Carlos ran out of the store that day. It was like a black cloud had settled on top of him, and he felt heavy for days afterward. He just didn't want to let Carlos down. He was everything he had.

"Yes, you did listen to Carlos. You listened to the music, to the movies, and everything else that quieted My voice. And pretty soon, you were able to leave Leslie and Sonya, and not think twice about it. That's why the spirit version you saw when you came here was so small, and your soul is so large." The Father motioned up and down. "Because that's what you've been feeding the last 24 years. But you weren't made of that material, Sonny. Deep down, you are kind, and that's why you spent your Saturdays cleaning up for Constance. That's why you convinced Carlos to get those shirts for Colleen, even though you stole them."

"Yeah," Sonny agreed. "But all that took a back seat when I had to survive."

"Survive?" the Father paused. "That's what so many of you all are focused on. Just surviving. And it was never supposed to be like that," the Father's eyes flickered with disappointment.

Sonny tried to make himself smaller. He knew he'd done some bad things during his lifetime, but he didn't know that he'd have to answer for everything all at once. The Father wrapped his arm around Sonny and continued.

"When you are not connected to Me, you don't know your purpose, and your whole life is reduced to survival. I'm not angry with you, Sonny," sighed the Father, yet sadness was painted in His eyes. "I'm disappointed because I had great plans for you. But all that has been forfeited.

"There was greatness inside of you, son." He tapped Sonny on the chest with His index finger, "but the thief ruled your life and kept you under that curse, even though I had provided a way of escape. His plan has always been to steal, kill, and destroy, and that's what he's done with five generations of fathers and children in your family."

It all became clear to Sonny. The curse was the darkness, fear, and loss of hope that had surrounded him. The curse had been the source of his aching emptiness that never seemed to really go away. Sometimes it quieted for a moment, but it was always lurking. And he had lived with its effect every day of his life.

Sonny took a deep breath as he connected the dots. He had rejected the Father and instead followed whatever he thought was right, which had now led him to this place. His children would grow up fatherless just like he had, and the cycle would continue.

"No, it won't continue," the Father's voice pierced the air. "Your daughter and son will be rescued by Paige and her husband. Paige couldn't reach you, but she is hoping to make a difference with your children. Would you like to see them?"

Sonny shrugged and got up to his feet.

"They will have the love, peace, and acceptance you were always looking for, and the prayers of Constance will finally be answered. Look this way."

* * *

Paige lay on the sofa and peered up at the ceiling. Her two little rug rats were in the other room and had finally settled down for an afternoon nap. She turned over to her side and thought about Sonya's bright eyes that lit up whenever she called her name. Then she thought about Josiah Junior helping Yuri with the dishes after dinner last night.

If someone so much as thought about running water in the kitchen, J.J. was dragging a chair up to the kitchen sink to help. "I help. I help," he insisted. The truth of the matter was that his help slowed down the dishwashing process. But Paige and Yuri loved to have his help anyway. In fact, they encouraged it.

Sometimes, Paige would wonder how they would make it all work. She and Yuri were newlyweds. Yuri was in law school, and they hadn't even been married a year. But when word came that Sonny was dead and his two children were going into the system, Paige talked to Yuri about getting custody. He'd agreed without even thinking about it. "We'll figure it out." Those were his exact words. "We'll figure it out." And Paige had fallen in love with him all over again.

Sonny's kids were her second chance. All she wanted to give them was a family—what the Sneeds have given her. Maybe she could help her brother's children, in the way she had always tried to help Sonny. Then she dozed off to sleep.

Minutes later, she heard Sonya screaming. J.J. had used her finger paint to cover their wall in green and blue. "Auntie look what J.J. did!" Sonya pointed at him and looked at Paige, expecting her to attack him.

"Come here, little fella. You didn't mean anything by it, did you?" she picked up the caramel-colored boy and nuzzled his curly hair with her face. "It's okay, Sonya. We can clean it up later. Want me to make you a snack?"

Sonya tumbled off the top bunk and nodded. The two braids, which hung down on each side of her head, bobbed up and down. Paige adjusted J.J. on her hip and took Sonya's little hand in hers.

"Uncle Yuri will be home soon to make dinner. So let's not eat too much, okay?"

"Okay," Sonya smiled up at her and followed her to the kitchen.

Sonny looked over to the Father and pointed to the little boy and girl. "Those are my kids?"

"Yes, and they will never have to worry about survival."

Sonny shook his head in disbelief. Paige was giving them something that he didn't know how to give—love and stability.

He tilted his head to the side and rubbed the back of his neck. He tried to process everything and figure out a way back. *But what about*

Leslie? Leslie had always been good to him, and she deserved a second chance too.

He had to get back. Yes, he'd seen his body murdered, but with everything else he'd also seen today, there must be a way. Surely, the Father could make some allowances, considering everything he'd been through. He simply had to figure out how to ask the question.

Then he felt a warm sensation on his left shoulder and turned slightly to see the Father looking down on him.

"Sonny, you can't go back. Your soul made an agreement with the curse by the daily choices you made. You never listened to My voice, and you made your choice. Leslie will be given just as many chances as you."

Sonny's chin dipped to his chest, and his strong shoulders dropped. He knew the Father was right. He had been given so many chances. But his turn had come and gone.

Squeezing his eyes shut, he said a silent prayer for his Leslie and his family, hoping that the blood would never spill on their shoes again.

THE END

A LETTER FROM THE AUTHOR

Since the early nineties, my family and I, as well as other advocates for fatherhood, have operated a mentoring program for fatherless boys. Sonny's story is fiction, but it is true. With this book, our goal is to give insight into the journey of a soul and address the consequences of a soul who is fatherless and disconnected from our heavenly Father.

We've seen Sonny's story many times over during the past three decades. We've cared for boys who have suffered mental illness, counseled young men who have witnessed brutal family murders, and prayed for victims of HIV/AIDS. The symptoms are different, but the root cause is always the same.

When a father leaves his children, emotional soul wounds—fear, rejection, and anger—take root. Some never heal. And many repeat themselves over generations. In the ancient Book of Malachi, the prophet admonishes:

> And he shall turn the heart of the fathers to the children, and the heart of the children to their fathers, lest I come and smite the earth with a curse (Malachi 4:6).

We see the effect of that curse on society every day—mass shootings, mass incarceration, police brutality, racism, and lack of compassion. We witness firsthand the disorder that results from the lack of father figures in this generation and also from the lack of father figures in previous generations.

The absence of loving fathers is the cancer at the core of our societal demise.

In *The Day Sonny Died,* you've read of the consequences caused by the absence of fathers, specifically, in the lives of our African American youth. And you've read how the cycle often repeats itself within a family.

In Ezra chapter 9, the prophet acknowledges the transgressions of the fathers and then calls the fathers to humble themselves and turn back to God. Fathers must renounce generational sins and break the power of those curses over their families.

It is through repentance, confession of sins, and forgiveness that the power of the transgression is destroyed. If there is no confession and repentance, however, the breach that was open through the sin remains open for future generations.

Just as the heavenly Father's only begotten Son, Jesus, forgave those who brutally murdered Him, people of African American descent must forgive those who have perpetrated the horrible crimes of slavery. As each family assesses the reality of Sonny's story within their own family, they should ask the heavenly Father what breaches have been committed among their own relatives, and break the power of the sin through repentance and forgiveness.

It is also crucial for Caucasian Americans, whose ancestors perpetrated crimes during the period of slavery and consequently opened breaches for sickness, death, and destruction upon their own families, to repent and ask the Father for forgiveness.

The good news for anyone is that there is a cure for any curse—our loving heavenly Father. He longs to know, provide for, and protect us… if we let Him. He loves us so much that He sent His Son to die for us and erase the yoke and pain of abandonment. For more information on getting to know your heavenly Father, please turn to the next page.

How to Know the Heavenly Father

God is our heavenly Father, and He is holy. Every soul on earth is given the opportunity to be reconciled back to the Father. We all have free will to choose. However, if you neglect the salvation that was purchased through the shed blood of Jesus and His resurrection from the dead, you reject Him.

The first step in getting to know Him is acknowledging that His Son, Jesus, took the punishment for your sins on the cross. Next, you must go before Him with a pure heart, turn from your faults—repent—and ask forgiveness. By acknowledging your faults and forgiving those who have hurt you, the weight of the pain will be lifted, and you will be restored to a relationship with your heavenly Father. When you forgive those who have abandoned, violated, or abused you, you close the emotional soul wounds and move toward healing.

As you repent, there will be a realignment. In this realignment, your soul submits to the spirit—which has been connected to the heavenly Father—and you are able to hear and discern the voice of God. In love, He continues to lead, guide, and direct every reconciled soul over the course of its journey here in the world.

Even though you can't see Him, your heavenly Father is always with you and knows how to rescue you when you call out to Him. His righteousness always goes before you in the midst of life's trials.

You can talk to your heavenly Father at any place and at any time. He is always present and waiting to hear from you.

December 17, 2015
Onnie I. Kirk, Jr.

READERS GROUP GUIDE

GENERAL QUESTIONS

1. There is an old adage, "The fruit doesn't fall far from the tree." This proverb is true. Whatever character is developed within the father, will be in his children. What similar characteristics did you recognize in Victor Senior, Victor Junior, and Sonny?

2. Constance, the Jackson family matriarch, had been abandoned by her biological family. Her husband then abused her emotionally and physically. And the rest of her hopes and dreams vanished with Rachel's pregnancy. Where did Constance find strength during life's hardships?

3. When a person's soul is wounded, he or she may seek comfort in alcohol, drugs, pornography, sex, money, power, stealing, and/or a host of other coping mechanisms. These coping strategies can be devastating to a family. What is the solution for healing from emotional soul wounds?

4. Sonny's sister, Paige, was adopted by a family who loved and cared for her. What impact did Paige's adoption have?

5. The heavenly Father took time, after Sonny entered the spirit world, to explain his past and give him a glimpse of the future. Why did He do that for him?

CHAPTER ONE – CHAPTER FIVE

1. Why did Constance internalize the fears, sorrow, and pain in her life?
2. How do you address the fear, pain, and sorrow in your life?
3. Where was the family support to help Constance in her time of need?
4. Why did Victor Senior suffer from panic attacks?
5. Who do you look to for guidance in your own life?

6. Does that person(s) exhibit the characteristics of your heavenly Father?

Chapter Six – Chapter Ten

1. Both Constance and Rachel had biological fathers who abandoned them. Who did they look to for guidance?
2. Rachel seemed to show little concern for her son or herself when the officer asked her if there was a relative who could pick up Sonny. Why was that?
3. When there is no biological or spiritual family support, who will be the rescuer in times of trouble?
4. When you were a child, who came to rescue you in times of trouble?
5. Why did Constance ask God for His forgiveness before she went to rescue Sonny?
6. How did God show up for Constance when she went to the Department of Children's Services?

Chapter Eleven – Chapter Fifteen

1. Constance told Sonny that Sister Bands' behavior was the "perfect example of living like an orphan." What was she trying to teach Sonny?
2. Why was Sonny excited to make the basketball team?
3. Carlos and Sonny became friends quickly. Why was Carlos's opinion so important to Sonny?
4. After the basketball game, Sonny was embarrassed about scoring the winning shot for the opposing team and angry with the twins. What was Coach Grimes trying to teach him about anger?
5. Athletics is often considered to be an antidote for today's troubled youth. While providing organized team interaction can be beneficial, why are there so many professional athletes who are violent and abusive?
6. Constance did what she could to prepare Sonny for his life, but he longed for his father. After his 13th birthday, she gave him a picture of his father and his grandfather's gold chain. Why were these keepsakes not enough to deter him from his destructive path?

CHAPTER SIXTEEN – CHAPTER TWENTY

1. Carlos had no moral boundaries in his life. His mother was neglectful, and his father was absent. His life experience had taught him to fend for himself and to use fear as a weapon. Why was Sonny drawn to him?
2. Mr. Young and Constance had something in common. After Carlos and Sonny stole from Young's Market, why didn't Mr. Young have them arrested?
3. Why was Deacon Michael so irritated with Pastor Andrews?
4. Rachel tried to numb the pain of her life with drugs, which led to prostitution. What unresolved issues led her to this lifestyle?
5. What issues do you need to resolve in order to move past the pain and embrace a life of peace and joy?
6. The trip back to the homestead brought back memories of Constance's childhood, and she hoped it would help Sonny appreciate where his family came from. Did he understand the importance of the trip?
7. When did Constance forgive her parents for abandoning her?
8. It is well documented that there are negative health consequences to unforgiveness: high blood pressure, anxiety, depression, and a weakened immune system. Do you have health challenges that could be related to unforgiveness?

CHAPTER TWENTY-ONE – CHAPTER TWENTY-FIVE

1. Paige's family was openly affectionate. Why was it easy for her to express her affection, but difficult for Sonny to respond?
2. What did it mean to Sonny when Anthony gave him dap and told him that he had "held his own"?
3. The adolescent years are difficult for a fatherless child. If there is no father to protect, provide, and help him discover who he is, the adolescent is forced to make survival decisions: joining gangs, prostituting, selling drugs. These subcultures offer provision and protection—in their misguided way—and often lead to a hopeless life of crime, imprisonment, and death. Do you know a young person who has lost his life as a member of one of these subcultures? Describe that person.

4. Sonny needed love and acceptance. How did this need effect his relationship with Carlos?
5. Constance taught Sonny that there were consequences for his actions, yet Carlos had grown up in an environment where the objective was survival. How did this mindset result in his death?
6. Why did Sonny escape death, even though there was a bullet hole in his hoodie?
7. After Carlos's death, Sonny got a tattoo. Why?
8. Leviticus 19:28 says: "Ye shall not make any cuttings in your flesh for the dead, nor print any marks upon you: I am the Lord." What does that mean?

CHAPTER TWENTY-SIX – CHAPTER THIRTY

1. Constance experienced many losses. What contributed to her stroke?
2. The thief seeks to steal, kill, and destroy, but our heavenly Father came that we might have life and have it more abundantly (see John 10:10). One of the thief's most devastating strategies is to remove fathers. How did this affect Sonny and Constance?
3. How has this strategy of the thief affected you?
4. No one prepared Sonny for real life, i.e. parenting, providing for a family, or the death of a loved one. The absence of family left Sonny without a foundation to build his life. He was alone with no one to protect or provide for him. James 1:27 says, "Pure religion before God and the Father is this, to visit the fatherless and widows in their trouble, and to keep himself unspotted from the world." Why didn't the church step up to care for him?
5. Sonny and Leslie loved each other, but both had voids in their lives. When Sonny lost the only guidance in his life, Constance, Leslie assumed the role. Why was Leslie so accepting of him?
6. What characteristics do good fathers demonstrate?
7. How have the characteristics of your father affected your life?
8. When people referred to Sonny's father, they referenced him as a great basketball player. That was his legacy. What legacy has your father passed on to you?

9. When Sonny heard his mother shouting in the crowd, it made him feel like he was no longer alone. But when Rachel announced that she was having another baby, how did this make him feel?
10. What can the church do to stop the cycle of fatherlessness?
11. Jesus, the Son of God, had an adopted father—Joseph. Joseph helped to provide and protect for Jesus as a child. Why was that provision and protection significant?
12. Because he'd never had a father to anchor him and teach him the responsibilities of a father, Sonny drifted. In time, his grandmother died. His mother couldn't be trusted. And his foster mother, Reesha, saw him as a paycheck. He was alone and afraid. How would you have felt in that situation?

Chapter Thirty-One – Thirty-Five

1. What happened to Sonny emotionally the day he "aged out" of foster care?
2. Sonny didn't know he was in a battle against generational brokenness. Meanwhile, Colleen's special treatment and attention messed with his mind. Before he knew it, he was abandoning Leslie. Why was it so easy for this to happen?
3. Thousands of children live under state-sponsored foster care. This artificial family set-up by the state can often do immense harm to the psychological and emotional development of a child. How did this system affect Sonny?
4. Why was it important for Sonny to buy shoes for his daughter?
5. There was a void in Leslie's soul, which sometimes made Sonny's abandonment and betrayal a nonissue. What had Leslie's mother really taught her?
6. Sonny pushed Paige away many times. Why was she still so loyal to him?
7. Sonny learned to survive, and with Leslie, he always had food and a place to stay. Why did Sonny use her?
8. Sonny never experienced the love and care of a father, and it affected how he saw God, the heavenly Father. When Deacon/Coach Grimes

presented Sonny with an opportunity to know his heavenly Father, what kept Sonny from surrendering?

CHAPTER THIRTY-SIX – CHAPTER FORTY

1. When Sonny was released from prison, he thought it strange that Leslie had not visited or tried to contact him. But when Rita explained that Leslie was in prison, Sonny was more concerned about himself. Why?
2. The emotion of rage is a dark force. When it enters a relationship, all moral and ethical boundaries are removed. Many times the person enraged doesn't remember the damage they caused. Have you been in a situation where rage triggered you to be violent or destructive?
3. If so, how did you cope with the aftermath?
4. To Rita, Sonny was a conquest. To Leslie, Sonny was her life. Why did Rita console Leslie?
5. When we die, our body returns to the dust. Our spirit returns to the heavenly Father (see Ecclesiastes 12:7). If we have been reconciled to God the Father through salvation, our soul returns with our spirit to be with Him. Sonny's spirit felt at home, but his soul had never been reconciled and did not know the Father. Knowing that Sonny's soul would be leaving soon, why did the Father spend so much time with him?

CHAPTER FORTY-ONE – CHAPTER FORTY-FIVE

1. Sonny did not know that the Father had placed an angel to help him, and on three occasions, his angel intervened to save his life. When have you experienced divine intervention in your life?
2. What patterns did you see repeat themselves over multiple generations of the Jackson family?
3. What patterns have you seen repeat themselves in your family?
4. Exodus 20:5b-6 says: "I the Lord thy God am a jealous God, visiting the iniquity [habitual sins] of the fathers upon the children unto the third and fourth generation of them that hate Me; and shewing mercy unto thousands of them that love Me, and keep My com-

mandments." How does this Scripture affect the societal landscape in America?

5. During his time with the Father, Sonny realized that he had been given multiple opportunities to be reconciled. In addition, the Father allowed him to glimpse the future of his children with Paige and her husband. Why was that significant?

SIMONE THANKS

First, I'd like to thank the Good Lord for keeping me sane through this entire process. The last four years have been filled with ups and downs, but my character is much improved. You, Lord, have given me peace despite the troubles.

Second, I'd like to thank My Darling Husband, My Patron of the Arts, and My Dance Partner for Life. Remember all those days I was dealing with the umpteenth rejection and wanted to quit? Thank you for not letting me. And for those days when I was procrastinating and finding a million other things to do...thanks for kicking me in the behind. Thanks for cooking dinner and washing clothes when I was in "the flow." Thank you for listening to my pieces even when you wanted to study Japanese. And most importantly, thank you for having the courage to tell me to do better because you knew that I could. I can't imagine a day without you.

Third, I'd like to thank the initial beta readers—Mom, Miriam, Issachar, Israel, Melba, Linda, Jan, Candie, Malcolm, Linda, Nicole, and Rob. The fact that you suffered through the cringe-worthy first draft is proof positive that you love us. Thank you, Jean, Tod, and Tim for reading the later drafts and for your support. Dad and I are so grateful. Y'all are a gift.

Fourth, I'd like to thank my friends for reading. It never ceases to amaze me that you *actually* read my work. There's just not enough words to express my gratitude. And thank you for cheering me on as I pursue this dream. Online writer friends, thank you for writing. Your words, encouragement, and acknowledgement of The Struggle comfort me daily.

Fifth, I'd like thank my writing buddy, Laura. Meeting you at ACFW was worth the cost of admission plus some. And to Beth...you said three simple words when I first met you, and it was the fuel I needed to keep going.

Finally, I'd like to thank Henry Bedford and the Southwestern Family of Companies. I can't think about your extraordinary act of generosity without tearing up. It was an answer to a prayer on so many levels, and I am forever grateful.

Love,

M. Simone Boyd
July 4, 2016
www.myfamilyfantastic.com
@msimoneboyd

ONNIE THANKS

Through my father's prayers and the foundation of love and faith that he lived, I am the man I am today. I can hear his voice constantly reminding me and my siblings to "keep our name clean." Born September 29, 1924, Onnie Isaac Kirk Senior was number 20 of 21 children. His parents were sharecroppers, and his formal education ended in the second grade when his father died and he headed to work in the fields to help care for his family. Christ came into his life at 33, and he learned to read. I believe he read the Bible every day of his life. He loved God the Father and his family. He was a living example of the integrity and taught us to always do what you say you will do. He was a man of strength and few words, and his legacy of fatherhood, faith, and character lives on in all of his children.

My wife, Margienell, is the love of my life. She's stood with me for 39 years and faithfully embraced our destiny. She is a woman of quiet strength and the mother of our eight biological children—three daughters and five sons. Each of them loves their family and are extremely supportive of each other. In addition to our biological children, Margienell and I have loved and cared for over 70 young men who had been growing up in homes where their fathers were absent. I'm grateful to Margienell for her heart to serve and sacrifice over these many years.

I am likewise grateful for our firstborn, Simone Boyd, a gifted writer who has so powerfully woven this tapestry of tragedy, sorrow, and pain into a portrait of hope as we choose to embrace the Father.

For Fatherhood,
Onnie I. Kirk, Jr.

eGenco

Powered by eGenco

Generation Culture Transformation

Specializing in publishing for generation culture change

Visit us Online at:

www.egen.co

Write to: eGenco

824 Tallow Hill Road

Chambersburg, PA 17202, USA

Phone: 717-461-3436

Email: info@egen.com

facebook.com/egenbooks

youtube.com/egenpub

egen.co/blog

pinterest.com/eGenDMP

twitter.com/eGenDMP

instagram.com/egenco_dmp

47611949R00122

Made in the USA
San Bernardino, CA
03 April 2017